One Wrong Turn

One Wrong Turn

CHENÉE MARRAPODI

FREMANTLE PRESS

'Dance, dance, otherwise we are lost.'
PINA BAUSCH

To Mum, for all the years of dance classes, competitions and sequin sewing.

1
Amelia

There's a feeling you get when you do ballet that's like nothing else in the world. Lots of people think ballet is just a hobby, something little girls in tutus do. They see a line of dancers standing at a ballet barre, slowly moving their arms and inclining their heads, and they think it's easy. What they don't see is the mechanics behind that arm movement. The discipline to make sure the arm bends in just the right way, that it's soft and delicate, yet strong and controlled. No one sees the muscles that are holding the rest of the body firmly in place so that hips don't wobble and bums don't stick out. No one sees that, because after all, it's just a hobby for little girls in tutus.

I'm fourteen and the novelty of tutus and tiaras wore off a long time ago. I know all about the blood, sweat and tears of ballet. If you aren't producing one or all of those three things, you aren't doing it properly.

As I performed a complicated piece of choreography for

my teacher, Miss Lily, I didn't think about the niggle in my hamstring that had been bothering me for the past month or the blister brewing inside my pointe shoe, threatening to pop – instead, my mind had wandered to another place. I was performing not just for my teacher, but instead for a sold-out crowd at His Majesty's Theatre. This particular dance wasn't pretty. It was powerful. I attacked each step like a lion chasing its prey, all the time keeping a cheeky smile dancing across my lips. Everything had to be precise and my timing had to be just right. The excitement tugged at my body, begging me to go faster. I fought against it. If I let adrenalin take over, I'd rush the dance and make a complete mess of things.

I finished the solo with a series of turns, travelling across the floor. In my head, I could hear the audience clapping in time with each turn and it spurred me on. As I reached the last one, I *relevéd* up onto the toe of one of my pointe shoes, trusting my body to hold me still.

I waited for the applause to come. Instead, there was silence.

The mirrored studio walls of the Perth Ballet Academy slowly came into focus. My breath burnt my chest as I glanced frantically around the studio. It was the best I'd ever danced, so where was the loud clap and recognition from Miss Lily? My eyes finally found her. She was standing by the door talking to a girl I'd never seen before. I didn't know who she was and quite frankly, I didn't care. She was interrupting my private lesson and had just made Miss Lily miss the best performance I'd ever done. It might not have been a *real* performance, but at a ballet school, every dance counted towards securing lead roles. Frustration surged through my body, eating up every last bit of energy I had.

Miss Lily glanced over her shoulder and saw me watching. 'Oh, Amelia, good, you're done.' It wasn't the praise I'd been hoping for. 'Come over here, will you. There's someone I'd like you to meet,' she said with a warm smile.

I straightened my shoulders and lifted my chin. I traded my scowl for a stage smile, knowing full well that a dancer with an attitude would get nowhere. As I made my way towards Miss Lily, I looked the other girl up and down. She was short and petite, and without a doubt a dancer. I could tell by the way she stood with her feet casually turned out and her neck poised.

The Perth Ballet Academy was one of the city's top ballet schools. You had to audition to get a place in its after-school program and it was unusual to see a new face midway through the term. Most of the kids in my class had been at the Academy since we were Juniors. As frustrated as I was with the interruption, curiosity got the better of me. I had to know who this new girl was.

'Amelia, this is Valentina. She's come to join us all the way from Italy. Her family moved here a couple of months ago and now she's settled in, she's dying to dance again,' Miss Lily said.

'I loved your dance,' Valentina said with a soft smile. 'It was incredible. Lots of energy.' Her accent was strong, but her English was clear.

'Valentina auditioned for me last week. You two are actually very similar. Two powerhouses,' Miss Lily said.

My smile tightened. I was the best Intermediate dancer at the Academy. Perhaps Miss Lily was just being polite, but with auditions for the midyear show just around the corner, the comparison between my dancing and Valentina's made me uneasy.

'Class starts in ten minutes. Valentina can shadow you today, Amelia, while she finds her feet. Make her feel at home, please,' Miss Lily said, heading towards the door.

I bit my lip. Babysitting the new kid was the last thing I wanted to do. I'm not like the other kids at the Academy. Everyone says they want to be a professional dancer, but sometimes it feels like I'm the only one working hard enough to make sure that dream actually comes true. I'm the first one at the Academy each afternoon and the last to leave, and from the moment I walk through the door, I'm ready to work. The others treat the Academy like a hangout, a place to chat and have fun, with a bit of ballet on the side. Not me. I'm 110 percent focused. I don't have time for distractions. Valentina included.

I wanted to protest against babysitting, but there was no point arguing with Miss Lily. Getting on the bad side of your ballet teacher was a sure way to land yourself in the *corps*, dancing in the background, waving a flower or some other lame prop – and no one would see you there.

'You're very good,' Valentina said, breaking the silence.

It was an olive branch, a peace offering, and of course, it made my chest puff out with pride.

'Thank you. It's the best solo I've ever done.'

'Perhaps you can teach me?' Valentina suggested with a hopeful smile.

I couldn't think of anything worse. I studied Valentina's face. Her eyes were warm and friendly. I didn't want to be mean. I know ballet has a bad reputation. Some people think ballerinas are snobs who go around sabotaging one another's careers, but it's not like that. At least not from what I've seen. I don't care about anyone else's dancing. I only care about my own. And it needs to be good. Better than good. With auditions coming up, my technique had to be flawless if I wanted to get the lead role. And I *had* to get the lead role. Every minute at the studio counted.

'Sorry, but I really need to practise my *pirouettes* before class,' I said. Last week, Sarah got her triple *pirouette* on pointe. She was the first one in our class to land it. I'd been working my bum off ever since.

'Great, I love to turn,' Valentina said, following me over to the mirror.

'Fabulous,' I said dryly. Clearly Valentina hadn't got the hint. I really just wanted to practise by myself. I took a deep breath and pushed off into a *pirouette. One, two,* I spun on my toe like a spinning top, keeping my eyes locked on my reflection in the mirror to stop myself from getting dizzy. On the third turn I began to wobble. I quickly planted my foot back onto the ground for balance and straightened up. My eyes darted towards Valentina. The last thing I wanted was to embarrass myself in front of the new kid.

Thankfully, Valentina was bent over, stretching her legs. I turned back to the mirror and this time, pushed off more gently. *Too gently.* Halfway through the second turn I realised I had nowhere near enough speed to make it around once more. I came to a stop facing away from the mirror, staring directly at Valentina.

This time, she'd been watching. 'Just a suggestion … and you do not have to listen,' she said, holding up her hands defensively. I could tell English wasn't Valentina's first language by how prim and proper her speech was. 'Do not' instead of 'don't'.

My jaw tightened.

Valentina continued. 'Maybe lift your knee a bit higher and bring your arms closer to your chest. Like that, you will have more … how you say … *forza*,' she blushed. 'Three turns will be easy, or as you Aussies say … *a piece of cake*,' at that she grinned, clearly proud of herself for knowing the saying.

'Have *you* got *your* triple *pirouette*?' I asked. It came out harsher than I'd intended.

Valentina smiled politely, but not before I saw the hint of a frown. '*Si*. Yes.' To prove her point, she effortlessly did a triple *pirouette*. She didn't wobble once.

I swallowed. Without a word, I turned my back and prepared for another *pirouette*. This time, I reluctantly took Valentina's advice. I drew my foot up a tiny bit higher and tightened my arms. *One, two, three!* As I softly placed my foot back on the ground, I released my breath and smiled. Valentina and I locked eyes in the mirror.

'That was incredible! Like that, you could have done four turns,' Valentina said.

The studio door flew open, interrupting the moment. The other dancers began to wander in. As usual, they were chatting loudly about their weekend plans, favourite TV shows, latest crushes. They were too busy gossiping to notice Valentina.

'We start at the barre,' I said, walking to my usual spot at the front.

Valentina followed awkwardly behind me. 'This school, it is very big. Much more pretty than my old school in Italy.'

'Look, Valentina,' I began. I wanted to warn her that Miss Lily hated talking in class. So did I. The chatterboxes always ended up in the back row.

'You can call me Vale.' She emphasised the 'e' as if it were the start of a word, like elephant or egg.

A loud clap put an end to the conversation.

'Intermediates, I hope you've warmed up your legs as well as your mouths,' Miss Lily said, sashaying across the studio. A few of the students giggled as they took their place at the barre. Miss Lily used to dance professionally for the Royal Ballet in London and even though she was now in her fifties, and kind of old, she still moved as if she was ready to take to the stage at a moment's notice. Today, her hair was styled in an elegant chignon and a long ballet skirt floated behind her. Despite her tiny frame, her voice boomed like a megaphone. 'If you haven't stretched, your legs will know about it later. We've got a lot to get through today,' she said, making her way to the music station. The speakers crackled angrily as she plugged her iPad into the sound system. It was well overdue an upgrade. 'I hope some of you have made an effort to introduce yourself to

Valentina. It's never fun being the new kid, so please don't just ignore her.'

The other kids started whispering, as if noticing Vale for the first time. Vale was smiling awkwardly, clearly hating the attention. I didn't blame her.

'We'll begin as we always do, with *pliés*. A demi- and full *plié* in first, followed by a *port de bras*, repeated in second, fourth and fifth, finishing with a beautiful rise on *demi-pointe*. Then we'll turn and do the other side. Valentina, just follow the others. You'll catch on fast enough,' Miss Lily said with an encouraging smile.

I straightened my shoulders and rested one hand lightly on the barre. The pressure was on. If Vale was going to copy me, I had to be perfect. She'd already seen me stuff up my *pirouette*s before class, I couldn't afford to make another mistake. As the soft introductory chords of the piano tinkled through the speakers, I felt a deep breath escape my lips. I hadn't even realised I'd been holding it in.

There's something really special about ballet. I can't figure out if it's the music, or the movements themselves, but whenever I'm dancing, I disappear into another world. It's like magic. Nothing else matters.

We moved quickly through each exercise. *Tendus, frappés, rond de jambes*. Miss Lily walked up and down the length of the barre throughout each exercise, correcting students as she went. 'Ava, we are doing ballet, not hula. Hips still please … Jessie, bottom in and lifting up, please. Imagine a string that extends from your head, pulling your entire body upwards. Liam, why does your hand look like a claw?' she paused near the front of the barre. I instantly felt my shoulders straighten and my stomach tighten. I could feel Miss Lily's eyes in my direction and I craved her attention.

'That looks great,' Miss Lily said. A smile crept onto my lips. 'Valentina, I'm so impressed by how quickly you're picking everything up.'

My jaw dropped and so did my shoulders. I could've sworn Miss Lily had been talking to me. Suddenly, I felt hands on my shoulders, pulling them backwards.

'Posture, Amelia,' Miss Lily said. With one finger, she tilted my chin up towards the corner of the room. 'Remember, no one wants to buy tickets to see a ballerina slouch across the stage.'

I continued to move through the movements as she adjusted my position, but inside, I was dying of embarrassment. Teachers always managed to look at the worst possible moment.

By the time we reached the final exercise of class, I was exhausted. We all congregated in two lines at the side of the studio, ready to do *grand jetés* across the floor. Sarah and

I were up first. We both leapt through the air in time with the music. I watched our reflections in the mirror, pushing myself to make sure my legs extended higher than Sarah's.

'Nice, Amelia. That extra stretching is paying off,' Miss Lily complimented. Flexibility's one of the things I always have to work at. Both my parents are ex-ballet dancers, yet surprisingly, I wasn't gifted with natural flexibility. I'm forever doing the splits with my foot resting on a stack of books to try and overstretch my muscles.

'Ah! Those *jetés* are the best I've seen in a *very* long time!' Miss Lily exclaimed.

I felt my grin grow wider. Finally, Miss Lily was noticing the extra work I was putting in.

'Everyone, look at Valentina's *jetés*!' Miss Lily continued. My smile dropped. Once again, the compliment hadn't been for me.

'Notice how her hips are perfectly square when she is in the air. Gosh, that flexibility! Incredible, those legs were *definitely* made for ballet,' Miss Lily said, clapping her hands.

Having reached the other end of the studio, I stopped to watch Valentina. Miss Lily was right. Her flexibility was next level. She threw her legs into the air with each *jeté*, not just doing the splits midair, but extending beyond them. I felt a fire burn in my gut. As hard as I worked, it was unlikely my legs would ever be like that.

'She's pretty amazing, huh?' Mei-Lin said, sidling up beside me.

'Mmm.'

'I was watching her during *grand battement* at the barre. Her kicks were so high, I'm surprised she didn't kick *you*.'

'Luckily, we avoided collisions,' I said. I watched as a few of the other girls gathered around Valentina, gushing over her *jetés*.

'Did you see her *arabesque*? She's *crazy* stretchy,' Ava added.

'I wish my legs looked like that!' Kate whined.

'You'd have to snap bones to get that flexible,' Ava said with a smirk. Kate gently shoved her shoulder in protest. Kate and Ava were best friends and without a doubt the biggest gossips in the entire school.

I turned my back on the conversation, pretending to watch the other dancers. If I had to hear one more time how flexible Valentina was, I'd probably scream.

'The competition's picked up, that's for sure,' Ava said.

'God, Amelia, I bet *you're* worried,' Kate said.

'What? Why would I be worried?' I asked. I avoided Kate's eyes, keeping my own fixed on the other dancers.

'Well, auditions are coming up for the midyear show. Imagine if the new girl came in and stole the lead,' Kate said.

It was a small comment, but it was like a match and it struck a fire inside of me. 'There's more to ballet than flexibility, you know,' I snapped, walking away from the barre to join the others. I heard Kate and Ava laugh behind me. I hated that they'd got to me and made me crack. It was what they did and why I tried to stay away from them.

We all clapped and curtsied politely as Miss Lily dismissed the class. While everyone else made a beeline for the change rooms, I grabbed a stretch band. My muscles were more pliable when they were warm and I'd never been more eager to work on my flexibility.

2
Valentina

By the time I got home from ballet I was desperate for some time out, but that was never going to happen with my family. We moved to Australia to escape the traditions of our tiny, old-fashioned town in Calabria but then moved to Balcatta and into what must be the most Italian street in Perth. One of Papà's cousins, Francesco, better known as Ciccio, found the house for us ahead of our arrival. It belonged to a friend of a friend of his and ticked all the right boxes – big block, vegetable garden and cheap rent. It also happened to be right next door to Ciccio's house.

Mamma hadn't sorted out her international driver's licence yet, so Ciccio's wife, Anna-Maria, picked me up from ballet in her battered, old hatchback. In typical Calabrese fashion, there was a crucifix hanging from the rear-view mirror and a bobble-headed Jesus sitting on the dashboard. The Southern Italians love their religious paraphernalia. I watched Jesus' head nod along in time to

Gianni Morandi's Greatest Hits as Anna-Maria gossiped about one of the other Italian families that lived in our street. Apparently, their daughter had started dating a kid that was covered in tattoos and based on that, Anna-Maria was pretty sure he was part of a gang.

Finally, as if Anna-Maria suddenly remembered what I'd spent my Saturday morning doing, she turned to me and asked, 'How was ballet? Are the Australians any good?'

'Very good,' I replied. I wanted to practise my English as much as I could, but it felt weird if Anna-Maria was speaking in Italian, so I didn't. 'The school's beautiful. It's huge. Much bigger than the one back home. There must have been at least twenty kids dancing with me today. There were only five of us at my old studio.'

Thankfully, Anna-Maria had returned her eyes to the road where she was navigating the hatchback as if it were a rally car. She had one hand on the steering wheel and waved the other around in the air as she spoke. 'Bigger isn't better. The Italians know how to do ballet. They're born with music in their blood and it comes out when they dance. The Tarantella? You know that dance? Italian. A girl, she was bitten by a tarantula spider and she danced to get rid of the poison. Now the whole world does that dance. All thanks to the Italians. Just remember, a big, fancy school doesn't mean anything.'

This from someone who had never danced a day in her life. Unless you count the family gatherings where the wine flows freely and the music is played at full volume.

Back in the Old Town, no one really understood my love of dance. Dancing was something you did as a kid. A hobby with an expiration date. Whenever I used to talk about my dreams of becoming a professional ballerina and performing at Teatro alla Scala in Milano, *i vecchi* – the old people – would just laugh and say I could dance around the house after my children. That was the expectation of the Old Town. Everyone was stuck in the past. According to them, the only thing I'd grow up to be was a mum.

We pulled up in front of Anna-Maria and Ciccio's house, then walked next door to our own. Judging by the number of cars outside, we had company. The Southern Italians have an open-door policy. If we're all from the same region of Italy, we're called *paesani,* meaning we're basically family and everyone's welcome. I kicked open the rickety front gate and followed the sound of voices to the backyard.

I found Papà playing Briscola against the other men. They slapped the coffee-stained cards down on the table and grunted if they weren't happy with the outcome. Occasionally, they were knocked by one of the kids doing laps of the backyard. You'd think we ran a day care. Anna-Maria's two youngest sons were there and so were my younger brother and sister, Giuseppe and Caterina. There were at least three more kids I didn't recognise, too.

The backyard was huge, much bigger than the tiny courtyard that surrounded our apartment complex back home. We had shared the complex with family. Nonna had lived on the bottom floor, Zio and his family on the second and us at the top. Here we had a whole house just for our little family. It was more space than we knew what to do with so, of course, we filled it with extra bodies.

I leant over Papà's shoulder, inhaling his familiar scent. It was a mix of his musky cologne, coffee and cigarettes. I flicked one of his Briscola cards. 'Play that one,' I said.

Papà smiled cheekily and slapped the card down on the table, winning the hand. The other men protested loudly.

'That's cheating!'

'Ballerina, you can't help him!'

I winked and stole an olive from a bowl on the table.

'Vale, make a pot of coffee for everyone, please,' Mamma called out from the clothesline. Unlike Papà, she was trying hard to only speak English. She still remembered a lot from when she used to live in the UK and sometimes, I could even hear the slight hint of a British accent. I thank Mamma for my English being so good. She knew English was our ticket out of Italy, so growing up she would read English books to me and speak the phrases she knew. My brothers and sister never showed any interest, but I loved the sound of the words so I lapped it up. Plus, with a big family it was always nice to get some special attention from Mamma. My English really took off when I found out you could watch blockbuster movies faster if you didn't wait for the dubbed version. The other kids at school were so jealous when I knew what happened in movies before they had even made it to the local cinema.

I grabbed another olive and wandered into the house to make coffee for everyone, dodging kids as I went. I found Nonna inside hunched over the stove, stirring one of the four pots that was bubbling away. As always, Nonna was dressed head to toe in black so that everyone knew she was still mourning my nonno. He died eight years ago, but in Nonna's mind, if she wasn't wearing black, other families might think she'd moved on. I tried to argue it once and told her that given her age, it was unlikely anyone would think she was going out on the town, prowling for men. She didn't much like that comment. I got a really long lecture about respect and another about the importance of *la bella figura* – making a good impression. Nonna was always worrying about what other people thought of our family.

'*Ciao*, Nonna!' I said. She didn't respond. She was in her late seventies and her hearing was starting to go. I repeated myself, louder this time. 'Nonna! *Ciao!*'

Nonna jumped and turned around. A smile lit up her face. She shuffled towards me and grabbed my face with both hands, planting multiple kisses on my cheeks. I felt the bristle of her whiskers against my skin. *'Ballerina mia!'* she said. Even though Nonna shared the view of *i vecchi* and wanted me to grow up, marry and pop out multiple kids, she secretly loved that I did ballet.

I asked her how her English was going. She rolled her eyes and swatted her hand in the air, batting the comment away as if it were an annoying fly. Nonna refused to learn English. She said she was too old and set in her ways. Plus, she only came to Australia because there was no one back home to look after her, so why should she learn the language?

I pulled out the aluminium coffee pot and began filling the base with water. Nonna grabbed it out of my hand and took over.

'Have you eaten? Get some pasta out of the pot. You're fading away with all that dancing,' she said.

I dished up a small bowl of pasta and took it to the table. Having placed the coffee pot on the stove, Nonna shuffled over, took my bowl and loaded more pasta into it. 'Not enough,' she told me. There was no point arguing, better just to eat what I could and give the rest to the chickens when Nonna wasn't looking.

My five-year-old sister Caterina came bounding into the room. She scrambled up onto my lap and snuggled into me while I ate. 'Did you dance on your toes today?' she asked.

'In English, Cate,' I said firmly. She had started school and was struggling to understand her teacher.

'I don't know the words,' she argued.

'That's why you have to speak English as much as you can. To learn them. I'll help you,' I said, eating a mouthful of pasta. As the tomato *sugo* hit my tastebuds, a hunger I didn't know I was feeling took over. I shovelled the pasta into my mouth.

'I want to be a ballerina too one day, Vale,' Caterina said, snuggling in to me. Our family had always been close, but since the move, Caterina had been extra clingy. We shared a room and I often found her curled up next to me during the night. The traffic was too loud for her and the streets were too wide. She missed her friends and the rest of the family back home.

'One day you'll be the best ballerina of all,' I said, planting a kiss on her forehead.

'Really?' Her eyes widened in disbelief.

'Definitely,' I said. I lifted her off my lap and carried my empty plate over to the sink. As I washed the sauce off, I thought about Caterina's comment. Being here in

Australia, maybe she would be a famous ballerina, or perhaps a scientist or an engineer. That's exactly why Mamma convinced Papà that we needed to come here. Opportunity.

'*Tesoro mio!*' Nonna exclaimed. Nonna's "treasure" was Salvatore, my older brother, who had just walked into the room. Based on how fast Nonna moved to smother him with kisses, you'd think the Pope had arrived. Salvatore hunched down to kiss Nonna.

I waved over at him. 'The King has returned,' I joked. Salvatore was another reason Mamma had insisted we left Italy. He had just turned fifteen and was running around town getting up to all sorts of mischief with the other boys. Not a lot had changed since we'd moved though. He was still never home, and here it was almost worse, because no one knew the city well enough to know where he'd be. Most of the time, he was with Anna-Maria's eldest son, so apparently that made everything okay.

'Are you hungry? I'll make *cotolette*,' Nonna offered.

'No *grazie*, Nonna. I'm going out. *Ciao*.' Just like that, Salvatore was gone. Again.

'*Cotolette*? I'd love some *cotolette*,' I said cheekily. For someone who wasn't hungry a minute ago, I suddenly had a huge appetite for Nonna's veal schnitzel.

'I don't have time. I'm cooking dinner,' Nonna said,

flicking her hand at me. Apparently the famous *cotolette* were reserved for *tesoro mio*.

The coffee pot began to gurgle angrily on the stove. 'The coffee's ready, take it outside,' Nonna said.

I shook my head as I placed the pot onto a tray with some biscuits. 'Does anyone care that Salvatore's never home?' I asked Nonna.

She just shrugged. 'Boys will be boys.'

3
Valentina

I got to the Academy early ahead of my second lesson. Amelia was already there, warming up at the far end of the barre. I smiled and nodded hello, but made my way to the middle of the barre. I got the impression Amelia wasn't my greatest fan. Today, I would do my own thing instead of trying to copy her.

I sat on the floor to put on my beloved pointe shoes. They were getting old and had started to soften with age. I knew I was due a new pair soon, but I wanted to soak up as much familiarity and luck as I could from my old pair first. New shoes were always stiff and took time to break in.

As I stretched, I watched the other students slowly drift into the room, most in pairs or groups, chatting loudly. My heart hurt watching them. I missed my friends back home and our constant chatter. Here, I felt like a mute. Until my English improved, I was too scared to speak more than I had to. I pushed the feeling of hurt away the only way I knew how. I distracted myself by stretching, focusing my mind on the soft pull in the back of my hamstrings as I reached past my toes. I closed my eyes and took three deep breaths, reaching a tiny bit farther with each one.

'So *you're* the new girl with the crazy flexibility?'

I opened my eyes and looked up to see a dark-skinned girl in a bright pink leotard staring down at me.

'I wasn't here last class, but *everyone's* been talking about you. That's right, you're Italian. I forgot. Sorry, am I speaking too fast?' she asked. She barely took a breath between each sentence. My family were fast talkers, but this girl spoke even faster than them. It was as if someone had pressed fast forward on a remote control.

I processed the words as quickly as I could and smiled. 'No, it is okay. I understand. I am Vale.'

'Oops, I'm Khalila. Should've said that, shouldn't I?' Khalila extended one of her long legs up onto the ballet barre as she spoke, reaching towards her foot. Her legs were at least a foot longer than mine. Italians aren't really known for their height.

I thought about what Khalila had said. How people had been talking about me. The comment made me uneasy. I wondered if they'd been laughing at the foreign girl who spoke with a thick accent. 'The other dancers ... they were talking about me?' I questioned.

'Nah, not like that,' Khalila said. She smiled and the

warmth of it melted my nerves away. 'They only said good things. Like how you're the most flexible person on the planet and that you turn faster than a fidget spinner. Oh, and you've made Amelia *insanely* jealous. But she'd never admit that,' she glanced over at Amelia and let out a giggle. It had a pixie-like tinkle to it. 'It must be *absolutely* killing her. I love it.'

'She is the most concentrated dancer I have ever met,' I said. As the words came out of my mouth, I knew they were wrong.

Khalila chuckled. 'Determined you mean. She is. She's harmless though. She's just obsessed with becoming a professional ballerina. It's those two you have to worry about.' She nodded towards two girls, one with hair as red as Nonna's tomato sugo. Before I had the chance to ask more, Miss Lily rushed through the door. The rest of the students took their places at the barre, ready to begin.

Miss Lily reminded me of my ballet teacher back home. She was warm and gentle when she spoke outside of class, but incredibly strict during. Maybe all ballet teachers were like that. I was desperate to impress her. I adjusted my feet into first position, squeezing my thigh muscles tightly together and rotating my feet outwards as far as they would go.

As the music began, I melted into a deep *plié*. I watched Khalila out of the corner of my eye. I liked her already. She was the nicest person I'd met since we'd arrived in Australia. She would fit in well with the girls at my old school. Although none of them would be caught dead in a leotard as bright as hers. The Old Town was pretty conservative. Black leotards, pink tights. Only the little kids wore bright colours.

I did my best to follow along with the exercises. Miss Lily taught quickly and everyone else already seemed to know what they were doing. Miss Lily corrected students throughout the exercises, but with the music playing loudly and my brain concentrating on the movements, I couldn't understand what she was saying. There was too much going on to translate at the same time. Thankfully it was enough to follow Khalila.

Miss Lily came up to me during one of the exercises. My arm was held out to the side in second position and Miss Lily gently rotated my elbow upwards. I hadn't even realised it had been drooping. She said something to me and I smiled and nodded politely, keeping my leg moving in time with the music. I didn't have a clue what she had said.

Khalila turned to face me between exercises. 'Girl, don't copy me in this one. *Frappés* aren't my thing. They're too fast and the change of direction gets me *every time*. I'm a *frappé* disaster.'

I was overwhelmed and the only thing I understood were the words '*frappés*' – which I knew was an exercise – and 'don't copy'. I nodded briskly. I'd do my best. I watched Miss Lily closely as she demonstrated the exercise, willing my brain to absorb it to memory.

The music began and I was relieved when I followed along easily. We were almost at the end when suddenly, Khalila's leg flew backwards as mine went forwards. She struck my foot, causing me to yelp in pain. My big toe throbbed but I forced myself to keep dancing. The last thing I wanted was to make a scene.

Khalila obviously felt differently. She spun around to face me, her hands framing either side of her face. 'O-M-G, I'm so sorry! I told you, I'm *completely* unco!' Khalila pranced awkwardly on the spot as she spoke.

'*Non ti preoccupare*,' I said, praying Khalila would keep dancing. The other dancers were looking over their shoulders, trying to see what all the fuss was about. I did my best to keep going and motioned for Khalila to do the same. She either didn't get it or didn't want to.

'Girls, everything okay?' Miss Lily asked, appearing by our side as the music came to an end.

'*Si*, okay,' I said, nodding. I could feel my cheeks growing warm.

'It was my fault,' Khalila said. She draped one hand dramatically across her forehead.

'No, é *stato colpa mia*,' I bit my lip, searching for the

words. 'My fault. My leg ... it went the wrong way.' I saw Khalila's eyes widen. She went to say something but I silenced her with a small shake of my head.

Miss Lily just laughed and waved her hand. 'Okay, we'll be careful. We don't want you breaking your toes in your first week,' she said with a wink, before walking back to the front of the class to explain the next exercise.

'Thank you,' Khalila whispered.

I just smiled. That's what friends did and I desperately wanted Khalila as a friend. I glanced around the rest of the room. Amelia was watching me from the front. We locked eyes briefly, before she turned back around to face Miss Lily. I groaned internally. Judging by Amelia's expression, she now thought I was a complete idiot. I wished I could tell her that it wasn't me who'd messed up, but that would mean embarrassing Khalila. I'd just have to prove myself in one of the other exercises.

I had my chance when it came time to do *pirouettes*. I memorised the combination Miss Lily gave us and performed it easily, turning this way and that, without a single wobble. Miss Lily applauded once we'd finished and made me do it again solo to show the rest of the class. I was so proud I felt like my chest might explode.

'See how Valentina pulls up high on her supporting leg and keeps her arms firmly in place as she turns. It's that strength that stops her from falling,' Miss Lily said once I'd finished.

Out of the corner of my eye I could see Amelia watching closely. Unlike the rest of the students, she wasn't smiling. Her lips were pursed in a tight line.

When Miss Lily excused the class, we all curtsied and clapped politely, before heading towards the change rooms. As I grabbed my drink bottle, I noticed Amelia was back in front of the mirror, once again practising her turns. She repeated the entire sequence from start to finish.

'That looked very good,' I said as I passed her. If Amelia heard me, she didn't say. She kept practising as if I hadn't spoken.

'Don't take it personally,' Khalila said, appearing at my side. 'I love ballet, but she's obsessed. A real Betty Bunhead that one.'

I wanted to ask what Betty Bunhead meant, but Khalila was still talking. I scurried after her towards the change room.

'She never stops dancing. Like, I don't think I've ever been at the Academy when she hasn't been here. I reckon she sleeps here.' Khalila said. 'One of the other girls was the first to get her triple *pirouette* last week and it's driving Amelia nuts that it wasn't her. Now you've come along and you spin like a propeller ... she'll probably cry herself to sleep tonight.'

I'd never met anyone who talked as much as Khalila. Which was a big call given I'm Italian and Italians love to talk.

High-pitched squeals echoed from the change rooms. We entered to find the girl with the bright red hair standing on top of one of the benches, triumphantly waving a purple bra in the air. 'A push-up bra!' she squealed between fits of giggles.

'Very funny, Ava, give it back, you moron.' A brunette girl jumped up on the bench beside Ava and wrestled the bra from her hand. 'You're just jealous.'

Ava shoved her, before climbing off the bench. 'I'm not jealous, I just don't need one,' she said smugly.

'Yeah. Right. When you need to upgrade your training bra, let me know,' the brunette said, before noticing Khalila and I watching. 'Oh hey! Ignore Ava, she's an idiot. I'm Kate. Sorry. I'm speaking too fast. HI … MY … NAME … IS … KATE.' She repeated her introduction in a loud voice.

People always did that. It was nice when people slowed down a tiny bit to make it easier for me to understand but, like that, it was so embarrassing.

'Her English is fantastic, Kate, and she's not deaf. You don't need to speak like that,' Khalila said.

'*Right.* How are you finding class? You're doing okay,' Kate said.

'Okay? She's nailing it. I've never seen anyone turn like that,' Khalila said.

It was like having my own bodyguard. I smiled gratefully at Khalila. 'Thank you. I like the Academy. Miss Lily is very good. She is hard, but good,' I said, pulling jeans out of my dance bag to change into.

'Auditions are coming up for the midyear show. Are you gonna be in it?' Ava asked, pulling pins out of her bun. She shook her head, releasing a cascade of red curls down her back.

'The midyear show?' I repeated.

'We do two shows a year. One at the end of June that's just for our class and some of the younger kids, and then one at Christmas time that involves the whole school, like the older Pre-professional students. The June show's *way* better because we're the oldest group in it, so we get to play the lead roles. Unlike at Christmas time when the Pre-professionals steal them all,' Kate explained.

'They hardly *steal* them all. They're just way better than us,' Khalila said.

'Whatever,' Kate said, rolling her eyes.

My mind had already started to wander. I pictured myself onstage, doing a series of *pirouettes* for a crowded theatre who, of course, would applaud as I finished and give me a standing ovation. The thought sent a shiver down my spine. If only.

4
Amelia

I raced up the stairs to the Academy, my feet barely touching each step. It was Saturday and after a long week of classes, Miss Lily had promised that today would be the day she announced what the midyear show would be. The suspense was killing me.

The Academy was like a ghost town and my footsteps echoed through the building. I was always early, but today, I was super early. I wanted extra time to warm up so that my body would be ready to tackle the new audition choreography. I dumped my bag in the change room and kicked off my sneakers, trading my warm tracksuit for even cosier warm-up gear. I pulled thigh-high knitted leg warmers over my ballet tights and wrapped a woollen cardigan around me. The warmer my muscles were, the more pliable they'd be and the less likely I'd be to get injured.

As soon as I was ready, I grabbed my pointe shoes and

headed to the studio. As I walked down the corridor, I could hear voices coming from Studio B. I frowned. I'd been at the Academy since I was three years old and no one had ever beaten me to class.

I peered around the door in case there was a private lesson in session. My heart sank. Valentina and Khalila were at the barre, rising up and down in their pointe shoes, chatting loudly. I made my way across the room to the far side of the barre. Valentina smiled at me and said, '*Ciao.*'

Khalila waved but carried on talking. Typical. She was the biggest chatterbox in the entire Academy.

I sat down on the floor to put my pointe shoes on, carefully sliding a protective pad over my toes, before pulling each shoe on.

'I'm not wearing toe pads today,' Khalila announced triumphantly.

I looked up. 'Why not?' Wearing toe pads was like having shields inside your pointe shoes. They didn't stop all blisters, but they definitely helped. Going without them would be like walking in a storm without an umbrella. Plain stupid.

'I heard some of the professional companies don't let the ballerinas wear them, so I thought I should start getting used to it now,' Khalila explained matter-of-factly.

I glanced over at Valentina to see what she thought of

the announcement. She looked about as dumbfounded as I felt. '*Ma no, non è possibile,*' she muttered to herself.

'Where on *earth* did you hear that?' I asked. If anyone should know what professional dancers could and couldn't do, it was me, and I'd never heard of such a stupid rule.

Khalila hesitated. 'I read it somewhere. Online. Apparently, it's so they can feel the floor better through their shoes.'

'Oh, you'll feel the floor alright,' I said sarcastically. If Khalila danced without toe pads though, it was unlikely she'd be able to feel the floor for very long. What she would feel, was a world of pain.

'This … does not sound like a good idea,' Vale said with a grimace. 'I think you will get many sores and bleed a lot.'

I nodded in support. Vale wasn't wrong. Blisters were an inevitable part of dancing on your toes, but it made sense to do what you could to avoid them.

'Oh, *come on*, it'll help build strength. You know how Miss Lily always says we need to strengthen our bodies for ballet,' Khalila said. As she spoke, she pointed one of her feet out to the side and pushed her weight over her toe, making a perfect arch with her foot. Khalila actually had beautiful feet for ballet. She had high arches and the curve made her feet look stunning when they were pointed. It was a shame she was too lazy to remember to point them while she danced though.

Dancing without toe pads was one of Khalila's more stupid ideas, but if she insisted on doing it, it was her funeral.

I silently warmed up, doing my best to block out Khalila and Valentina's chatter. Khalila, of course, carried the conversation, with Vale only contributing small phrases here and there. Given English was her second language, I was impressed she could understand Khalila at all. Khalila barely paused long enough to catch her breath.

'Hey, bunheads! Who's ready to find out which prince I'll play this year?' Sam Collins said, bursting through the studio door with a couple of the other boys in tow.

Vale and Khalila laughed. I groaned. Sam was one of the better male dancers at the Academy and he knew it. He was arrogant and always eager to show off. To be fair though, there was only a handful of boys at the Academy and most were still going through the awkward gangly stage, so the chances of Sam getting the lead male role were pretty high.

'Maybe instead of a prince, you'll be a toad this year,' I said, balancing on one leg as I spoke.

'Very original,' Sam said, flicking me with his sweat towel as he walked past.

I wobbled and lowered my leg. 'Hey! That better have

been clean!' I called after him.

Sam looked back at me and winked. 'You should be so lucky, bunhead.'

I scowled. Why did boys have to be so gross? Sam and I had danced together for years. We used to compete together in *pas de deux*, or duo competitions. I was always a princess and Sam was always my prince. He was sweet when we were young, then his teenage hormones hit, he grew muscles and became a bit of a jerk.

'I hope we're doing *Snow White*, or *Sleeping Beauty*. I'd love to be Aurora,' Khalila said. She leant against the barre, daydreaming about the different roles she'd like to play. Dreams I knew were unlikely to come true. There was no way Khalila would get a lead róle. She spent more time talking in class than she did dancing, and as a result her technique wasn't anywhere near where it should be. Miss Lily was always telling her she needed to take class more seriously, so there was no way she would be trusted with a lead role.

I was hoping Miss Lily would choose *Don Quixote*. It was one of my favourite ballets of all time and I already knew one of the main solos. It was a really hard dance so I'd be a shoo-in for the lead. There was no one else strong enough to perform it. At least, there wasn't anyone before Valentina arrived. I glanced at her out of the corner of my eye. Valentina was a really good dancer. I'd be lying if I said it didn't make me nervous. The only thing working in my favour was the fact that Miss Lily probably wouldn't give the lead role to a new kid. Valentina hadn't done her time. She hadn't proven herself like the rest of us had.

People might think I'm silly for being so obsessed with getting the lead, but ballet is my whole life. I dance, sleep, eat, repeat. And do my homework, of course, but more often than not, dance comes first. I'm at the Academy every day except Fridays and Sundays. I work every single muscle in my body until it's at breaking point. If I'm not getting the lead roles, then it's all for nothing.

The air grew thick with nerves and excitement as the Intermediate and Junior students congregated in the studio. Altogether there were at least forty of us, all eagerly awaiting Miss Lily's arrival. The older dancers sat chatting in groups, each predicting what the midyear show might be. The younger kids played tag, running circles around the older students. I screwed up my nose in disgust. They were acting like they were at the zoo.

Two little girls sat quietly together beneath the ballet barre. I smiled. They looked just like me and my best friend Alice used to when we were little. Alice was just as desperate to become a professional as I was. We always trained together, stretching one another's legs, pushing each other past our usual limits. We had so much fun. Then a couple of years ago Alice moved away. Her dad got a job in Singapore and the whole family went with him. No one else had been able to take Alice's place. No one else took class anywhere near as seriously as we had.

I glanced up at the little white clock on the wall. It hung on an angle above one of the mirrors and always ran six minutes fast. I counted backwards. Class should have started two minutes ago.

Finally, Miss Lily sashayed through the door. 'Okay everyone, gather around!' she announced, clapping her hands loudly for attention. A wave of excitement rippled through the room and we all quickly formed a semicircle around her.

I knelt down in the front row, desperate to hear what the show would be. Vale and Khalila shuffled in beside me. I kept my eyes straight ahead. Focused and ready.

'The midyear show's just around the corner and I know you're all going to love this year's story,' Miss Lily said.

My heart pounded in anticipation. What would it be – *Don Quixote, Coppélia, Swan Lake*? Out of the corner of my eye, I noticed Khalila had her eyes closed, mouthing something. I bristled. Khalila was always doing weird stuff and her lack of focus irritated me. I turned to look at her properly and realised she was mouthing the words

'Sleeping Beauty' with her fingers crossed. I rolled my eyes and turned my attention back to Miss Lily.

'I'm excited to say, this year we'll be performing … *Cinderella!*' Miss Lily announced with a smile. Excited whispers filled the room.

A wave of goosebumps rippled along my arm. I remembered watching my mum perform Cinderella when I was just a little girl. Looks aren't everything, but based on Disney's version, my blonde hair and blue eyes made me perfect for the part.

Starting today, we had one week to perfect the audition choreography, then we'd perform it individually for Miss Lily and another teacher, Mr Michael.

'Well, I've already got the Prince in the bag. Later, bunheads!' Sam said, getting up to leave.

'Not so fast, Sam,' Miss Lily said. 'I want you and the other boys to go to Studio A. Mr Michael's waiting there to teach you your audition piece.'

'Doesn't the Prince have a servant or a slave or something? Maybe you're better suited to one of those roles,' Khalila said, patting Sam on the shoulder.

Sam screwed up his face at Khalila, before following the other boys out of the studio.

Vale tapped me on the shoulder. 'Um, what does it mean, "bunheads"?'

I let out a small laugh. It was a funny name and I'd never really given it much thought. 'It's stupid, really. A bunhead is someone who's obsessed with ballet. Bun ... head,' I said, pointing to my hair. 'He thinks he's funny. He's not.'

Vale laughed, her whole face lighting up. 'Is there a boy bunhead?'

'Yep, his name's Sam and he's an idiot,' Khalila interrupted.

I shook my head with a laugh and used the opportunity to escape. I positioned myself at the front of the class, where Miss Lily would be able to keep a close eye on me as I learnt the audition choreography.

A few steps in and I realised it was much tougher than I'd anticipated. My calf muscles protested as I *relevéd* up and down on my toes. The individual steps themselves weren't overly difficult, but the dance was long and some of the steps were repetitive. It was easy to get confused and forget which part you were up to. I raced to keep up with the chords of the piano.

'Faster girls! You all need to buy watches. You are completely out of time,' Miss Lily yelled over the music.

I pursed my lips and dug deeper. This wasn't even the audition, but the thought of Miss Lily thinking I wasn't good enough killed me. I sucked my stomach in tighter, willing my muscles to hold me firm. It's a funny concept to explain to someone if they've never done ballet, but if I let my gut and bum hang out, keeping my balance would be near on impossible. I needed every muscle in my body to be working, but the trick was, I couldn't let anyone else *see* how hard I was working. A good ballet dancer makes sure their movements look completely effortless. It's one of the toughest things about ballet.

There was one person who wasn't trying to hide the effort one bit. Khalila. Behind me she was grunting and groaning with every step.

'Khalila, we are doing ballet, not playing tennis. There is absolutely no need for that noise every time you move,' Miss Lily said as she walked between the rows. 'Ballet is supposed to look graceful. We want people to think dancing on our toes is the most natural thing in the world.'

I smirked and glanced over my shoulder.

Khalila forced a smile that more closely resembled a grimace. 'Yes, Miss Lily,' she grunted.

Next to Khalila, Vale was doing her best to keep up with the steps. She stepped up onto her toes and lifted her arms high above her head into fifth position.

'Beautiful, Valentina, now soften those arms a bit,' Miss Lily said, adjusting Vale's arms to make them more rounded.

I turned back around. I couldn't let myself get distracted.

I began the combination again, watching myself closely in the mirror, analysing the position of my hips and the angle of my arms. I had almost reached the end of the combination, when Khalila let out another loud grunt. I came down off pointe and turned around. 'Will you keep it down,' I hissed.

Khalila smiled sheepishly.

'*Tutto bene*?' Vale said. Khalila and I stared at her with raised eyebrows. 'Sorry, everything is okay?' Vale repeated.

'It's like … knives … in my shoes,' Khalila spluttered between steps.

'What?' Vale asked.

Honestly, how was I expected to perfect the choreography with these two clowns carrying on behind me?

'Knives. It's like there are knives in my shoes, trying to cut off my toes,' Khalila repeated.

The comment made me laugh. Served Khalila right for not wearing toe pads.

'Perhaps it was a bad idea not to wear the toe pads,' Vale said.

Khalila took a deep breath and kept dancing. 'I'm sure it just takes getting used to. No pain, no gain. Right?'

'Eh, *si*, but a ballerina in pain is not so pretty,' Vale said with a grimace.

I laughed. She had a point. When Miss Lily finally

announced the class was over for the day, Khalila let out a loud cheer. Miss Lily shot her a look of disapproval. I rolled my eyes. *So unprofessional.*

'Please, *please*, practise everyone. It's hard choreography. The audition is next week. I want all of you to do your best,' Miss Lily said as she left the studio.

'Finally, I can take these damn shoes off,' Khalila said, hobbling towards the side of the room. All of the students milled around the studio, chugging water from their drink bottles and pulling their shoes off.

I stayed in front of the mirror, going over the choreography one last time to cement it into my brain. Even with all of the students chatting, it was impossible to block out Khalila's foghorn voice. I watched her closely in the mirror. She was such a drama queen.

'I'm not gunna lie, it hurt a bit today. But it'll get easier, I'm sure,' Khalila said, gingerly pulling off one of her shoes. She let out a small gasp as she saw her toes.

'*Oh dio!*' Vale said, staring at Khalila's feet in horror.

Khalila looked like she'd seen a ghost. The toes of her pink ballet tights were stained with blood.

'I told you it felt like knives,' Khalila said.

'This is … very not good,' Vale said.

I headed for the studio door, pausing as I passed Khalila. 'So it went well I see – dancing without toe pads. I bet the floor felt really good,' I teased.

Khalila dropped her bottom lip sulkily. Vale laughed and patted her on the shoulder.

I was halfway out the door when I heard Khalila say, 'God, I hate it when Amelia's right!'

5
Amelia

'Professional dancers can wear toe pads right?'

It was the first thing out of my mouth as soon as I climbed into Mum's car to go home. I didn't believe Khalila, but part of me still felt the need to double-check.

'Hi Mum, how are you? Did you have a good day?' Mum said, imitating my voice. Why do parents do that? It's so annoying.

'Sorry. Hi, Mum. How are you?' I grumbled.

'I'm great, thanks for asking, love!' she said with a giant smile. I rolled my eyes. 'Now, what were you saying about toe pads?'

'Professional dancers can wear them, right?' I stared out the window as we pulled out of the Academy car park. Vale was standing on the kerb surrounded by a couple of the other girls. She was chatting animatedly, her hands moving faster than her mouth.

'Of course they can! Gosh, I'd stuff all sorts of things into my shoes to dull the pain. You don't get a medal for bravery. It's more of a survival thing,' Mum said.

I nestled back into my seat, relieved. After seeing Khalila's feet, I had no desire to part with my toe pads.

'I peeked through the studio door earlier. Is that the audition chorey?' Mum asked.

'Yep,' I replied. I hated it when Mum watched class. Parents weren't allowed, but Mum acted like being an ex-dancer gave her special privileges. It didn't.

'You looked good. Hard choreography I see. You should try –'

I cut her off. 'Mum, you shouldn't watch class. You know Miss Lily doesn't like it.'

'Oh, don't be silly,' Mum said with a wave of her hand. 'She doesn't mind every now and then. No one even saw me. What I was going to say, your *arabesque* –'

'Mum, we were just learning the choreography. I was marking. I know how to do an *arabesque* properly.' It's hard having a ballet dancer for a mum. Most other mothers would watch a ballet step and tell their daughter how beautiful it looked, even if it was executed horribly. Not my mum. She picks apart every single step. Just once I wish she'd notice the things I did well, instead of all the things that needed improving. It's exhausting. People probably think it's Mum forcing me to dance. It's not, I love ballet more than anything in the world. Mum just adds a whole other level of pressure on top of what I already put on myself.

'You know, it wouldn't hurt to at least listen to my advice every now and again. I do know a thing or two about ballet, you know,' Mum said.

Silence hung in the air. I used the opportunity to run over the audition steps in my mind.

'You didn't tell me there was a new girl. What's her name? Where did she dance before?'

'Valentina. She's from Italy.'

'Oh, an Italian! They have some great ballet companies in Italy. She's quite good. Very precise with her movements. I see Sarah's getting taller and taller. Poor love. She'd want to hope she doesn't get much taller. Tall ballet dancers are hard to match with a partner for *pas de deux*. It never looks right when the male is shorter than his partner. It makes the lifts look completely wrong,' Mum said.

Here we go. Now we'd have to go through every person in the class and point out their strengths and weaknesses. If only the car had an eject button so I could remove myself from the vehicle.

'Did I ever tell you about the first time your dad and I danced together?'

I yawned. Only about a million times.

'He was dancing Romeo and another girl, Louise – was

it Louise? Maybe it was Katherine. Anyway, she was meant to be dancing Juliet, but she was just too tall. The directors thought it would be fine when they chose the casting, but in rehearsals, it looked terrible. Your poor dad – you know he's not the tallest man – well, he struggled to lift her properly. She looked like a giraffe.'

Was Sam taller than Valentina? Surely, Vale was tiny.

'So, the directors decided they cared more about your dad being Romeo than Katherine … Louise – whatever her name was – being Juliet. So, they switched her role and made me Juliet. The rest is history. Perfect love story, isn't it?' Mum's eyes sparkled as she relived the memory.

'Great story,' I said dryly.

'You are so rude sometimes,' Mum said, playfully slapping me on the thigh.

'Ow! I'm joking, geez. It's very romantic. You and Dad. Match made in ballet heaven.'

We finally pulled into the driveway. 'You didn't tell me, what's the midyear performance?'

'*Cinderella*,' I said, shoving the car door open, desperate to make an escape.

'Oh *Cinderella*! I love *Cinderella*. You'd make a wonderful Cinderella – if you work on those *arabesques*. I danced Cinderella so many times. Did I tell you about the time I –'

I slammed the car door shut and raced into the house

before Mum could keep going. I loved ballet, but I didn't need to spend all night reliving 'the good old days'.

Sometimes the house feels too quiet. That's the hard part about being an only child. There's no one to share the attention with so I'm either completely smothered by my parents or I'm lonely. It's true I like to be by myself at ballet, but that's only so I don't get distracted. By the time I finish class and get home from the Academy, it's like there's this ball of energy bouncing around inside me, desperate to jump out.

When I was younger, I had begged Mum and Dad for a younger sister. They always said 'maybe one day'. Every kid knows that that means no. Then one day I overheard Mum talking to a ballet friend of hers, saying how much she hated being pregnant – how sick it made her feel and how hard it was to get her body back into shape to dance again afterwards. She laughed and said there was no way she'd ever go through that again. From that moment on, I gave up asking for a sister. Alice filled the gap for a while, until she left.

We live in a small house, nothing fancy, but ridiculously clean. Mum is a neat freak. Dust makes her crazy. There's not really a lot of money in ballet, so we aren't exactly swimming in cash. Dad's an accountant these days and Mum teaches dance at a local school, but as they always tell me, all their money goes on my dancing. Regular classes, private lessons, pointe shoes, costumes … things add up pretty quickly. Knowing that, even if I didn't have my heart set on becoming a professional dancer, I'd still feel heaps of pressure to take things seriously.

There is one really cool thing about our teeny tiny house – the garage. A couple of years ago, Mum and Dad converted it into a studio so I had enough room to rehearse at home. The concrete floor was covered with sprung wood and mirrors were hung up along one wall. Needless to say, the cars now live outside on the driveway. When it comes to my ballet, no expense is spared.

With nothing else to do, I headed for the garage as soon as I got home. I might as well get in a bit more audition practice. It didn't take long before my calves were absolutely killing me. No surprise given I'd already done a couple of hours at the Academy.

'Don't you think you've done enough today?' Mum asked, peering around the door.

'One more time,' I said. There was a tiny step that I kept muddling up.

'No, that's enough. Your body is tired. You need to listen to it.'

I glared at her. I could never win with Mum. One minute she was telling me I needed to work on my *arabesques*, the next, she was telling me to take a break. I sighed dramatically so that she knew I was irritated, before heading towards the door.

'Ballet's not going anywhere, Amelia,' Mum said. 'You can practise again later.'

I rolled my eyes as soon as Mum was out of sight. I grumpily headed towards the kitchen in search of Dad. I was disappointed to find him on a work call at the kitchen table. He had about a trillion files full of numbers spread out in front of him and he was busy explaining to someone why it was impossible for them to claim something on tax.

I'd never admit it to any other kids my age, but my dad's kind of cool. He's not intense about ballet like Mum. I've actually questioned a couple of times whether he ever really was a dancer, because he's one of the clumsiest people I've ever met. How he never dropped and broke his *pas de deux* partner is beyond me.

Dad spotted me watching him and waved, signalling he'd only be a minute. I grabbed myself a glass of water and brought one over for him, too. He finally hung up the call and took a long swig of water before he spoke.

'Ah! Thanks, kiddo. I needed that. Some phone calls go

forever. That one could've just been an email.' He placed the glass on the table and in typical Dad fashion, somehow managed to knock it over. Water gushed out across his files. 'Ah, bugger,' he said sheepishly.

I grabbed the glass just in time before it rolled off the edge of the table. 'I'll get a tea towel, shall I?'

Dad nodded, busy shaking water off his files. 'Where's your mum?'

'Well, she's just finished giving me a lecture on ballet, so now she's probably digging out old videos of her dancing Cinderella.' I said.

'Do I want to ask?'

'We're doing *Cinderella* for the midyear show,' I said, dabbing at the spilt water with the tea towel. 'Mum's taking a walk down memory lane. It's painful.'

'I was a great Prince, wanna see me dance?' Dad said. He did a tiny jig, then laughed and winked. 'Just joking. Despite my amazing diet and exercise regime, this body isn't what it used to be. Hey, wanna go for ice-cream?'

'Is ice-cream part of that amazing diet you were talking about?' I asked with a laugh. 'I'll come. But only if we can sneak out before Mum finds out.'

'Before Mum finds out what?' Mum said, appearing in the doorway. She had supersonic hearing.

'We're going for ice-cream. Wanna come?' Dad said.

'Rob, we had ice-cream the other day. Twice in one week? Isn't that a bit much?'

I rolled my eyes. We really should have snuck out before she appeared.

'It's the diet of champions. Let's go!' Dad said, grabbing his coat.

'It is winter you know,' Mum said, reluctantly following behind.

'It's barely winter,' Dad argued.

I tossed the tea towel into the sink and headed for the door. Mum paused, grabbed the tea towel and hung it over the oven handle. She just couldn't help herself.

Within two minutes of eating my ice-cream, the guilt began to set in. I should've been home practising for the audition. Was I crazy? I only had a week. This time last week I'd been a lot more relaxed about the whole thing. This time last week, I didn't really have any competition. Now Vale was at the Academy, everything had changed.

'What's up, kiddo? You're eating ice-cream and you couldn't look more miserable,' Dad said, taking a giant lick of his pistachio ice-cream.

'I'm just thinking about the audition,' I said. Outside, the temperature was only twenty-one degrees, but I was eating my hazelnut ice-cream so slowly that it had begun to melt.

'You work so hard. I wouldn't worry,' Dad said. He was the most carefree person on the planet. He and Mum were polar opposites. 'What will happen, will happen.'

'Your dad's right,' Mum said.

That's a first, I thought. Mum never coped with how relaxed Dad was about things.

'If you just practise hard, work on your *pirouettes* and your flexibility, you'll be fine,' Mum said.

'Simple as that, huh?' I asked.

'You know what I mean,' Mum said. 'As your dad said, you're a hard worker. Miss Lily knows that.'

'The new girl's really good,' I said. I moved my spoon around in the cup, not really feeling much like eating anymore.

'Ah, so that's what this is about. New competition on the block, huh?' Dad said. 'Competition's good. It keeps things fresh and exciting.'

Exciting was a funny word to use. Stressful, maybe. High pressure, definitely. Exciting? Not really. Then again, if I wanted to be a professional, competition came with the territory. 'I'm just tired, that's all. I'll be fine once I go over the chorey some more,' I said, chucking my half-eaten ice-cream into the bin. 'It would all be a whole lot easier if you home-schooled me so I could join the Academy's full-time program.'

Dad groaned. 'Not that again.'

'Oh, come on. You both know how competitive ballet is and how hard it is to get into a company. I should be dancing more,' I said. We had the same argument at least once a month. Given the reaction I got every time, you'd think my parents hated ballet.

'And we also know how unreliable it is. Injuries, funding cuts, broken contracts … you need to make sure you have something to fall back on,' Mum said.

'You didn't and you turned out fine. If I don't make it into a company …' I gulped at the thought. 'I'll teach ballet, like you do.'

'We're not having this discussion again. You're too young to go full-time,' Mum said.

'But –'

'Enough,' Mum said firmly.

'Speaking of school, how's that English essay coming along?' Dad asked.

I groaned. 'It's coming …'

'It best be. How about getting that finished now before you get back into audition prep?'

'But Dad …'

'No buts. You know the deal, kiddo. Dance as much as you

like, we won't stop you, but you can't let your school work slip. We aren't asking for straight A's, but we do expect hard work.'

I rolled my eyes. Was there any such thing as work that wasn't hard?

6
Valentina

I hadn't stopped practising since Miss Lily had announced the audition. Miss Lily's style of choreography was very different to what I'd learnt back home and I wanted to make sure everything was perfect. I had a lot to prove. I felt like people underestimated me because I was new and my English wasn't always correct. With my broken sentences and stupid mistakes, they acted like I was uneducated, when if they spoke to me in Italian, things would be completely different.

At least when it came to dancing, language didn't matter as much. Ballet was about emotions and expressing them through movement. I could tell an entire story without uttering a single word. I didn't expect to get a lead role in *Cinderella*, I just wanted to go into the audition and prove I wasn't useless. I wanted people to know my school in Italy had taught me a lot, even though it was small and the building was falling apart.

I practised whenever I could – in the kitchen, in the garden, wherever I could steal a tiny bit of space – which was hard given the size of my family and the numerous visitors we always seemed to have.

'Your daughter doesn't stop dancing,' Ciccio said to Papà. It was eleven o'clock at night and they had just returned home from Ciccio's restaurant, where Papà was working as a chef.

I was dancing up and down the hallway. It was the biggest space I could find without there being furniture in the way. I paused and kissed both Papà and Ciccio on each cheek to say hello.

'*Si*, my ballerina doesn't stop. Have you studied today?' Papà asked. His eyes looked tired. He worked late almost every night at Ciccio's restaurant.

I nodded. I had studied as soon as I got home from ballet. That's why I was practising so late.

'Good. Remember, it's nice to dance, but there's no future in nice,' Papà said. He shook Ciccio's hand and said goodnight.

I frowned. Papà didn't get it. It was like the idea of me being a professional dancer one day was impossible for him to grasp. Perhaps if I did well at the audition, he would understand I had talent and that this wasn't just a hobby.

I rose up onto my pointe shoes and winced. My lucky shoes were getting too soft. It was getting harder and harder to hold myself up on my toes. If they got too soft, it would be impossible and I could hurt myself.

'Papà,' I said quietly.

'*Si, principessa*,' he replied. He rubbed his temples and yawned. Now probably wasn't the best time to ask him for new shoes. New pointe shoes were expensive and they didn't last long.

'Don't worry. It's nothing. See you tomorrow,' I said. I ran through the dance one more time, waltzing the length of the hallway. The house was old and the owners had left a chaotic assortment of artwork on the walls. I stopped in front of a small religious frame that was particularly strange. It was one of those fancy pictures where the image changed depending on which side of it you stood. From the left, it was Jesus, from the right, it was Mary. The only problem was, it was ridiculously old, and if you stood in the middle, all you could see was Mary with a beard. Salvatore and I had laughed at it so much when we'd first moved in that Nonna had told us off for being disrespectful. Now in the dim light, it was more creepy than funny.

'Vale, you need to sleep,' Mamma called out, appearing at the end of the hallway.

'One more time,' I said.

'Not today. You have school tomorrow. Your brain won't work.'

There was never any point arguing with my parents. I'd never win. Plus, one more *relevé* and my shoes would die for sure. I at least needed them to last until after the audition. I slipped off my shoes and was just about to head for my bedroom, when the front door opened. Salvatore came in. I didn't even know he'd been out.

'Where have you been?' I asked.

'Fatti i fatti tuoi.' Salvatore was only a year older than me, but being a boy, he had a whole different set of rules. Back home, men were the superior sex.

'You're dancing again? It's all you ever do,' Salvatore said.

'As you said, mind your own business.' I replied, heading for my bedroom.

I crept into the room, careful not to wake up Caterina who was snoring quietly in my single bed. I pulled on my pyjamas and slid in beside her. She groaned, then nuzzled in, sighing contently. It was the fourth night in a row that she'd insisted on sleeping in my bed. For such a tiny person, she moved around a lot, making it impossible to sleep. The night before I'd given up and climbed into her bed, only to find her back next to me twenty minutes later. She wasn't coping at pre-primary. That afternoon she'd told me one of the kids had teased her because she had accidentally called their teacher mister instead of missus. I wanted to find that kid and punch him. He had no idea how hard it was to move country, change schools and learn a whole new language. Poor Cate. My family was my entire world.

Well, my family and ballet. The thought of anyone hurting my sister made me burn with anger.

The day before the audition, Khalila came to my house for one last practice. It was a Friday, the only night of the week we didn't have ballet class. I'd wanted to go to her house to escape the insanity of my family, but Mamma was reluctant. She didn't know Khalila and she didn't feel comfortable sending me to a stranger's house. If I were Salvatore, I wouldn't have even had to ask.

Papà was already at the restaurant and Mamma, Anna-Maria and Nonna were busy making lasagne for the weekend. As usual, Anna-Maria was carrying the conversation, telling an animated story about the latest scandal that she'd heard fresh from the Old Town.

I glanced out the window, waiting for Khalila to arrive. Giuseppe and Caterina were playing in the front yard with Anna-Maria's boys. Caterina was crying because the boys wouldn't let her kick the football. I headed out the front to help her. They protested loudly as I caught the ball mid-flight and passed it to Caterina.

'Vale, no. She doesn't know how to play AFL!' Giuseppe cried in Italian.

'Neither did you a month ago,' I said.

'That's not true. I knew,' Giuseppe argued.

I playfully pinched his ear. 'You did not and you should be speaking English.'

Caterina kicked the ball, sending it wobbling into a bush. Giuseppe groaned and ran off to fetch it.

A car pulled up in front of the house.

'Hey, girl! You ready to dance?' Khalila called, waving her mum goodbye.

Caterina stood shyly at my side, hugging my hip. 'Always!' I said with a smile. 'This is Princess Caterina. She will be the best ballet dancer there is one day.'

'Really? I can't wait to watch you dance,' Khalila said.

I felt Caterina loosen her grip. 'Your hair ... it is pretty,' she said quietly in English.

'So is yours! And you're so clever speaking English,' Khalila said, making Caterina beam with pride.

'That is my brother and cousins,' I said, waving my hand towards the boys.

'Big family! Like mine. Exhausting, huh?' Khalila said, following me inside. Caterina let go of my hand and took Khalila's. It was funny how easily little kids made friends. Seeing Caterina with Khalila made me question why she was having such a tough time at school.

'I have an older brother, too. Salvatore. He is not here. He is allowed to do what he wants.'

Khalila raised her eyebrows in question.

'Because he is a boy. Girls stay home, tend to the house, boys do what they like. That's the Southern Italian way,' I explained.

'Really? Sounds old-fashioned. I thought Italy was the same as here? Girl power and all that,' Khalila said, punching her fist into the air.

'Ah, *si*. The rest of Italy is more like that. But my town is very small. In the mountains. We have maybe only three thousand people and everyone is very traditional. That's why we left,' I said with a wink. 'To be free.'

'Well Dorothy, you aren't in Kansas anymore and I'm very glad. The Academy is way more fun with you there. Although, I wanted to punch Amelia in her smug face yesterday in class,' Khalila said.

I laughed. 'She is not bad.'

'Not bad? Did you see her roll her eyes when I accidentally got in her way? And she's such a know-it-all. Always sucking up to Miss Lily. The worst part is Miss Lily thinks the sun shines out of her bum.'

Khalila spoke like no one I'd ever met before. She was so loud and honest, with the funniest sayings. 'That is because she is a hard worker. But yes, she is very … competition,' I said.

'Competitive,' Khalila corrected. 'Girl, there's one thing

we need to fix with your English. You're always so formal. If you wanna be Australian, you have to be lazier when you speak. No more "that is", "she is", "it is". We say "that's", "she's", "it's", Khalila said, clicking her fingers as she rattled off each phrase.

'Got it. Be lazy. *It's cool, girl,*' I said, impersonating Khalila's voice.

Khalila laughed, then stopped suddenly, raising her hand to her chest dramatically. 'What is that amazing smell?' she said, sniffing the air.

'I think you mean, *what's that amazing smell*?' I said cheekily.

'You learn quickly. Now, what's that amazing smell? It's making me weak in the knees,' Khalila said.

Caterina tapped her on the shoulder. Khalila bent down so that Caterina could whisper in her ear. 'Mamma is cooking the lasagne.'

Hearing Caterina trying so hard to speak English to Khalila gave me goosebumps. I couldn't have been prouder.

'You know what? It's the best smelling lasagne I've ever smelt,' Khalila whispered back to Caterina, making her giggle.

'Are you hungry?' I asked. 'Do you want something to eat before we dance?' I was desperate to start dancing, but the unofficial Italian laws meant I couldn't risk Khalila starving to death during her visit.

'Nah, I'm good. It just smells yum. Let's dance!'

We passed through the kitchen on our way to the backyard. With the other kids out the front, it was the area with the most space.

'Oh, hello!' Mamma said, a ladle full of sauce in her hand, ready to top the lasagne.

'Hi Mrs … Valentina's Mum,' Khalila said. 'Sorry, I don't know your surname.'

'Giorgi,' I said.

'Mrs Giorgi,' Khalila said. 'The lasagne smells delicious!'

'Are you hungry?' Anna-Maria said. 'Vale, get your friend something to eat.'

'She is not hungry. I checked,' I said defensively.

'No, no, I'm okay. We're here to dance,' Khalila said, shaking her hands to emphasise she didn't want food.

Nonna pottered away at the stove, boiling pasta sheets, glancing up occasionally to eye Khalila suspiciously.

'Have some cheese,' Anna-Maria said, cutting off a chunk of mozzarella and holding it out to Khalila.

'If the girl says she doesn't want to eat Anna, she doesn't want to eat,' Mamma said with a shrug. They were my words, not hers. I was always telling her to stop forcing food down people's throats.

'It's just a piece of cheese,' Anna-Maria said, her hand still extended to Khalila. Caterina suddenly jumped forward and snatched the cheese, giggling as she munched down on it. 'Brava, *bella mia*. See, the cheese is good.' Anna-Maria said.

Khalila laughed. 'Okay, I'll have some cheese. *Grazie*,' Khalila said. She winked at me. 'I've been practising my Italian. Although, a friend's cousin taught me a lot of swear words and I don't think your family would like that.'

Khalila took a piece of cheese and we quickly raced outside before any more food could be offered. 'Ergh, you know what else Amelia did?' Khalila said.

'Do not worry about Amelia!' I said, throwing my arms into the air.

'*Don't*. But she's so annoying! I swear she laughed when Sarah stuffed up the choreography.'

'Sarah laughed too,' I said. I had already begun to run through the audition steps, pointing my feet as hard as I could in my sneakers.

'That's not the point. Amelia shouldn't have laughed. We can't all have ballet dancers for parents and be as perfect as she is,' Khalila said. She joined in the dance and together we did ballet across the back patio. Caterina danced behind us, raising her arms into the air, copying the best she could.

'*Brava Cate*,' I said. 'Amelia's parents, are they really dancers?'

'Yes. Well, not anymore. They used to be. For the West Australian Ballet. No doubt they secretly train Amelia to make sure she gets all the lead parts. I heard she has her own studio in her house.'

'I think your imagination is very ... hyperactive,' I said. I muddled up one of the steps and stopped with my hands on my hips. *'Mannaggia!'* I grumbled. I couldn't concentrate on the dance if I was trying to speak in English at the same time.

'Overactive. Although yes, you might be right, I am a bit hypo too. And no, I'm not imagining things. She's evil. I can't stand that she was right about the toe pad thing. How was I supposed to know it would be like dancing with my feet in a paper shredder? Maybe she should be cast as the Evil Stepmother. She wouldn't even have to act,' Khalila said, kicking her shoes off. 'Sorry, do you mind? I can't dance properly in sneaks.'

'I don't mind,' I said, although the thought of dancing barefoot on the dusty pavement grossed me out. Caterina quickly kicked her own shoes off. I think Khalila had a new fan. 'You are ... *you're*' – I said pointedly – 'being mean. Amelia is not that bad.'

'I'm not, you're just new to the Academy and everything is sunshine and rainbows for you. Anyway, it makes no difference what I think of Amelia, she'll still be given the lead role,' Khalila said. She flopped down onto one of the patio chairs. 'Show me the dance. I'll critique. Then we'll swap.'

I nodded and slowly began the dance. 'Maybe she deserves the lead. She is the hardest worker I have seen in my life.' Concentrating hard on the words, I forgot the dance and had to return to the beginning. *"Mannaggia!"*

'Well, yeah,' Khalila said. 'But Miss Lily has her favourites.'

'Huh?' I said. I stopped dancing. It was too hard to do both.

'It's a ballet school. Teachers have their favourites. The same people get chosen for things … you know, to stand in the front line, dance the solo part …' Khalila trailed off.

I knew she was right. Italian dance schools … even Italians in general, were no different. Sometimes who you were and who you knew mattered more than the work you did. It sucked if you were a nobody.

'Just don't get your hopes up, that's all I'm saying. Now stop talking and dance,' Khalila said, pulling her legs up onto the chair.

I laughed. 'You talk more than me!'

'Watch me now!' Caterina said suddenly, holding her arms above her head and spinning in a circle. Khalila and I laughed and I stepped to the side. I was happy for Caterina to have a turn in the spotlight while I processed everything.

'Anyway, even if neither of us gets the lead role, there are plenty of other cool characters to play,' Khalila said. 'We could be the Stepsisters!'

'I think you and I look very different,' I said with a grin.

'You're right. You're much too short,' Khalila said, winking. 'Okay, maybe we can't both be the Stepsisters. But there's the Fairy Godmother, the Evil Step Mum, the Prince's Assistant, the Ball Guests, the Mice –'

'The Mice?'

'*I topi?*' Caterina echoed loudly.

'Yeah, the Mice. They help make Cinderella's dress in the movie,' Khalila explained.

'*Che schifo!*' I said. 'That is disgusting! But thankfully, I do not think the mice are in the ballet.'

'Well, that's disappointing,' Khalila said. 'At least you'd get to be onstage a lot. They were always scampering around in the movie.'

We practised until the steps were burnt into our brains. Mamma forced us to stop for dinner, then we went straight back to it. By the time Khalila left and I climbed into bed, my brain was in overdrive. I knew I was lying to myself when I said it didn't matter if I got a lead role or not. I was good at the choreography and I felt like I could play Cinderella. But was that even an option if Amelia was the favourite?

By the time I fell asleep, with Caterina curled at my side, there were a thousand mice in pointe shoes, dancing through my dreams.

7
Amelia

I lied when I said I didn't care about anyone's dancing except my own. What I actually meant was I didn't care about anyone else's dancing, so long as mine was better. Particularly on audition day.

I was last on the list to perform for Miss Lily and Mr Michael. At first, I was happy when I saw the running order. At least going last, my performance would be fresh in Miss Lily's mind when she was making her decision. But as it turned out, having to wait until last meant I had way too much time to stress myself out.

I was meant to be warming up in one of the small studios like everyone else, running through the steps over and over again to make sure there was no way I could possibly get them wrong. Instead, something had pulled me towards Studio A's second entrance. No one ever used the door and from there, I could watch everyone else's auditions and suss out the competition. I crouched down low and peered through the door, which I had quietly cracked open. I'm not sure why I did it. It's not like it would change how I danced. Regardless of what I saw, I would go into my audition and dance the best I could to secure the lead role. Within the next few hours, I would be named Cinderella.

Ava had almost finished her solo. From what I could see, she'd done a pretty good job. She'd only made one small mistake, the rest had been fine. Probably not good enough to land a lead role, but maybe one of the supporting ones.

The audition piece had been choreographed for pointe shoes, but Miss Lily had warned us that some of the roles would either be performed in soft canvas shoes, or a bit of both. Apparently as Intermediates she didn't think we were strong enough to do an entire production in pointe shoes. No doubt that comment wasn't directed at me. My feet were tough and my ankles were even stronger than some of the advanced students'.

I drew in my breath as Vale walked into the studio. She looked confident. I'd only known Vale for a short time, but it was clear, she was my biggest competition. I had to keep reminding myself that Vale was new and she hadn't proven herself. There was no way Miss Lily would give the lead role to someone who had only danced at the Academy for two seconds.

Miss Lily said something and Valentina laughed. I leant in closer to the door, desperate to be in on the joke.

'Getting a good show?'

I jumped at the sound of Sam's voice. I could feel the heat rising into my cheeks as I searched for an explanation. There was no reason for me to be at the door, other than to spy. 'I haven't been here very long,' I whispered. A complete lie. I'd watched every single audition from start to finish.

Sam laughed. 'Yeah, whatever, bunhead. It's good to know what you're up against,' he said with a shrug.

'Don't call me that,' I said stubbornly. I hated the term bunhead. It made it sound like everything I was working towards was some kind of a joke.

The opening chords of *Cinderella* began to play. I quickly shuffled back towards the door. I flinched as Sam rested his hand on my shoulder, peering through the crack above my head.

'Hey, watch it,' I hissed. 'And haven't you ever heard of deodorant?'

'Damn, she's good,' Sam whispered. 'Italy makes good dancers. And pasta. I love pasta.'

I glared through the gap in the door, willing Valentina to make a mistake. I hated myself for thinking like that, but watching Valentina, it was impossible not to. Sam was right, her performance was incredible. So far, not a single mistake and her stupid flexibility made everything look a million times better than average.

The final *pirouette* would be the tell-all. Miss Lily had left it up to us to decide whether we did a single, double or triple turn to finish. So far, everyone had played it safe with either a single or a double. Jessie hadn't even managed that. She'd been so nervous that she'd made a complete mess out of a single turn and ruined her entire audition.

I held my breath. Not surprisingly, Valentina chose a triple *pirouette* and it was flawless. My heart sunk. It would be a hard audition to beat.

'Ha! She nailed it,' Sam said, standing up straight as soon as Valentina curtsied and left the audition room.

'She was alright,' I said, trying to hide my panic. This wasn't how the auditions were supposed to go. I reminded myself again that Valentina was new. There was no way Miss Lily would give me the flick for her. I pushed past Sam and headed for Studio C.

'Done spying then?' he called after me.

I glanced over my shoulder and with fake bravado said, 'I'm going to warm up. Prepare yourself for a real show.'

I closed my eyes and waited for the music to start. This was it. My one shot. As the opening chords of the piano began to play, I plastered on my stage smile and took my first steps as Cinderella.

The studio became Cinderella's house. I was cleaning while daydreaming about the Prince's Grand Ball. Performing is different to the exercises we do in class. As much as I love doing them, the exercises are repetitive. Even when the combination changes, the basics remain the same. It's all about perfecting technique and sometimes it feels more like bootcamp than dancing.

When you're performing, everything changes. Technique is still important, but it's not always your brain that's controlling the movement. The music gets into your body and adrenalin takes over. For me, everything becomes a blur and sometimes it feels like my body has a life of its own.

Usually, I'm happy for impulse to take over. But not in an audition. I couldn't risk losing myself to the moment. I had to focus and make sure every tiny step was perfect. I pointed my feet harder than I ever had, tightening every single muscle in my body. I picked up the prop broom and swept the floor, waltzing this way and that, making a show out of pretending it was the Prince, as he and I shared our first dance.

I snuck a quick peek out of the corner of my eye. Miss Lily and Mr Michael were smiling. It was one of those encouraging smiles where you can never really tell if it's real or fake. My stomach fluttered as Mr Michael wrote something on his notepad. What had he written? I was certain I hadn't done anything wrong.

I forced my attention back to the dance. I couldn't afford to lose focus now. I placed the broom down and prepared for the final steps. All that was left was a quick series of jumps, followed by the last *pirouette*. I dug even deeper, drawing out every bit of energy I had tucked away. I jumped higher than I ever had before, beating my calves together to make my feet look like butterfly wings, fluttering in the air. Coming to a stop, I sunk into a deep *plié*, preparing for the *pirouette*.

All of a sudden, my mind began to race. I had less than a millisecond to decide whether I would do a double or a triple *pirouette*. Up until now, I'd been planning to play it safe and stick to a clean double, but Vale had raised the stakes. Time was up and I pushed off, my decision still unclear. I spun once, then twice. My balance was perfect, my bodyweight was exactly over my big toe where it needed to be. It was now or never. I sucked in my stomach tighter and took the risk. Halfway into the third turn I knew I'd made a terrible mistake. As my balance wavered, I dropped my heel and spun the rest of the way around on a flat foot, before jamming my other leg back down onto the floor to stop myself from falling over. My knee jarred and my heart sank. I had just blown the entire audition.

I forced myself to smile as I waited in my finishing position. I was hoping that if I pretended everything was okay, Miss Lily and Mr Michael wouldn't realise the mess I'd just made.

Time stood still. They both scribbled in their notepads. Every little part of my audition was being analysed and recorded. I studied Miss Lily's face, but I couldn't tell what was going through her mind. If she were to look up, I wondered whether she'd be able to tell what was going through mine. The fact that in that very moment, I was doing all I could to stop myself from bursting into tears.

'Thank you, Amelia. That will be all,' Miss Lily finally said, looking up with a smile.

I stepped to the side and curtsied politely. As I made my way out of the studio, I made sure my shoulders were back and my chin was tilted upwards. The stage smile didn't leave my face until the door was securely closed behind me.

Frozen in the hallway, I replayed the past two minutes in my mind. Surely I was overreacting. Surely my *pirouette* hadn't been as horrible as it had felt. Surely one little mistake wouldn't cost me the entire audition. I glanced back at the studio door. Maybe I could walk back in and ask for a redo. Miss Lily had practically known me since I was in nappies. If anyone could feign having an off day, or feeling unwell, it was me. She would know it was completely out of character and understand. Even as I thought it, I knew it wasn't a possibility. You didn't get a redo when it came to auditions.

I slowly made my way down the corridor, going over and over the audition in my mind. I could hear the chatter drifting out of the change room and I wished I didn't have to go in. Everyone was recapping their auditions. I didn't know what I'd say if they asked me how I went. As I stepped through the door, the room fell silent. Everyone turned to face me.

'Amelia! How did you go? Why am I even asking? Perfect I bet,' Mei-Lin said.

I paused, then plastered back on my stage smile. 'Really well,' I said with a shrug. I couldn't let anyone know what had happened. I wondered whether they could tell, whether perhaps my pounding heart was giving me away.

'Lucky you,' Jessie said flatly. She was sitting on one of the benches with her arms wrapped around her knees. Her eyes were bright red and her cheeks were stained with tears. I bit my lip. At least it was a triple turn I stuffed up, not a single.

'Miss Lily said the casting would be announced in an hour. I can't believe her and Mr Michael are in there right now, talking about us all,' Khalila said, gazing blankly at the ceiling.

'Do not think about it,' Vale said. 'You will become crazy.'

'I'll go crazy if we sit here for a whole hour. Let's go to the cafe downstairs and get milkshakes,' Khalila said, springing to her feet and grabbing her bag.

Vale laughed and followed her towards the door. She paused as she passed me. 'You can come?'

'No,' I replied quickly. 'Thanks.' I couldn't think of anything worse than sitting with Khalila and Vale, discussing the highs and lows of the audition. Vale's perfect *pirouette* and my disaster. I could pretend everything was okay for a short time, but if anyone asked too many questions, I'd break.

'Suit yourself. Come on, Vale,' Khalila said, dragging Valentina out of the room.

As the change room began to clear, I sunk down onto a bench and tugged off my pointe shoes. I couldn't believe I'd been so stupid. The number one rule of *pirouettes* was to be decisive, to know exactly how many turns you wanted to do before pushing off. Thank god Miss Lily knew me better than anyone else. She knew what I was capable of. Sure, I'd stuffed up the end of my audition, but Miss Lily knew she could rely on me for anything. Right now, she and Mr Michael were probably laughing about how out of character my mistake had been. The two of them were probably shrugging it off, knowing it would be a shame not to give me the lead over such a random, silly mistake.

I pulled on my tracksuit and made my way to the green room, crossing my fingers that no one else had decided to wait there. Thankfully, the Academy was like a ghost town. Everyone must have gone to the cafe. I grabbed a dance magazine and curled up on an old grey couch. I flicked from page to page, looking at the images but not seeing a thing.

The beep of my mobile phone made me jump. I glanced at the screen.

<MUM: How did you go?????>

I ignored the text and kept flicking through the magazine. My eyes landed on an article titled *Perfect your Pirouette*. I groaned and tossed the magazine back onto the coffee table. Sometimes the universe was really cruel.

Five minutes later, the phone rang. I contemplated hitting decline, but knew Mum would just keep calling until I answered.

'Hello.'

'Honey! You didn't respond to my text. How'd you go?' Mum's voice screeched in my ear.

I bit my lip. 'Sorry, just finished. It went well,' I said, trying to make my voice sound as chirpy as possible.

'That's great, honey! Did Miss Lily look impressed?'

I didn't know what to say. Finally, I settled with, 'Yeah, super impressed.'

'And what about the final *pirouette*? Did you go with a double or triple? I know you were worried about that bit,' Mum pushed.

I rubbed the back of my neck and stared at the ceiling. 'Triple,' I said and then without a second thought quickly added, 'and I nailed it!' I made a face at the phone. *I wish.*

'I wish I'd seen it. I'm so proud of you! Good luck with the casting. I know you'll do great. We can celebrate tonight. Whatever meal you want.'

I swallowed as I hung up the phone. At least someone was confident I would do great. Time couldn't move any slower. I bet the other girls weren't anywhere near as stressed out as I was. They had probably already moved on from audition talk and were busy chatting about reality TV or something just as stupid.

I leapt to my feet the minute Miss Lily emerged from her office holding the casting sheet. The past forty-five minutes had felt like torture. I had replayed the audition a million times in my mind and seesawed between thinking my life was completely over and the possibility that I was overreacting.

Miss Lily was fifteen minutes ahead of schedule, so the Academy was still quiet. I'd be the first to see the casting list. I hung back as Miss Lily pinned the sheet of paper to the noticeboard. I was suddenly radiating heat. I flapped the bottom of my tracksuit jacket, trying to let some air flow through. I had to be Cinderella. There was no other option.

Miss Lily turned and gave me a small smile, before retreating back to her office. I tried to decipher her smile, trying to figure out if it said *congratulations, great work*, or *better luck next time*. Miss Lily always gave us time to process the casting. She wouldn't speak to anyone about the results until Monday.

As if in a trance, I glided towards the noticeboard. I felt physically sick. When I reached it, I closed my eyes and took a deep breath to steady myself, before reopening them.

When I did, I couldn't believe what I saw.

8
Valentina

'The suspense is killing me,' Khalila said, dramatically slumping back in her leather seat. We were nestled in a booth at Maggie's, the cafe below the Academy. We had made a deal not to discuss the audition while we were at the cafe. For Khalila, that had lasted all of two minutes.

'We are not thinking about it. Remember?' I said, raising my eyebrows.

'We're,' Khalila corrected. '*We're* not thinking about it. Only, it's *all* I can think about.'

Her constant corrections were annoying, but I wanted to sound like a local, so as Khalila said, I had to suck it up. Khalila couldn't sit still. You could practically see the nervous energy buzzing through her body. She swung her legs back and forth beneath the table, drumming her fingers on its surface.

'*Dai* … keep still! You are exhausting me,' I said with a laugh.

Khalila huffed but stopped moving her hands. For a

moment, I thought her body was finally still, but then I felt a sharp kick hit my shin. 'Uffa!' I yelped, rubbing my leg under the table. 'What happened to keeping still?'

'Sorry,' Khalila said sheepishly.

A waitress appeared with our drinks. Khalila had tried to convince me to have a milkshake, but in my family, milk was for breakfast. Nonna said it was too hard to digest later in the day and we'd end up sick if we drank it. Milkshakes weren't even on the menu in the Old Town! The waitress placed a glass of orange juice in front of me and a caramel milkshake in front of Khalila.

'You're missing out,' Khalila said as she took a big slurp of her milkshake.

'If my nonna saw you drinking that, she would die.'

'You'd better not tell her then,' Khalila grinned. She wiped her mouth with the back of her hand and looked thoughtfully out the window. 'Trust Amelia to blitz her audition.'

'Are you really surprised? She does not stop practising.' I had come out of my audition feeling confident. Everything had gone to plan and Miss Lily and Mr Michael had seemed impressed. I didn't think that really mattered though. I kept reminding myself of Khalila's warning – *Miss Lily had her favourites*. I was too new to make that list.

'You don't have to be so nice, you know,' Khalila said.

I stirred my juice with my straw, watching the fluffy bits of orange float around the glass. 'I'm not. It's true.'

'If you ask me, she's been a cow to you ever since you started,' Khalila said between slurps.

I took a sip of my juice. It wasn't completely true. Amelia hadn't said a single nasty thing to me. She just hadn't really made an effort. She'd probably got caught up in the audition hysteria. Just like all of the other students at the Academy. Myself included. 'No, that is not true. She is just focused. That's all.'

'Whatever,' Khalila snorted. 'Just wait until she gets cast as Cinderella. You think she's a diva now, we'll probably have to start curtsying every time we see her.'

'*I* do not think she is a diva. And *you're* just being dramatic,' I said.

We weren't the only ones to escape the Academy while we waited. The majority of the other kids were at the cafe too, huddled in groups, laughing and chatting about the audition. I locked eyes with Ava and before I could look away, she stood up and walked towards us.

Khalila groaned. 'She's like the sun, Vale. You're not supposed to look directly at her.'

I stifled a laugh as Ava reached our table.

'Wanna hear some goss?' she asked, leaning against the

table with one hand, the other on her hip. I had no idea what "goss" meant. I stayed quiet, hoping it would become clear as the conversation continued.

Khalila scrunched up her nose. 'From you? Nah, not really.'

I smiled uncertainly at Ava.

'Trust me, *you'll* wanna hear this,' Ava said. She lowered her voice so that Khalila and I had to lean in closer to hear. 'I heard, from a very reliable source, that Amelia's audition wasn't as perfect as she made out.'

I glanced at Khalila. She had her head cocked to one side like a curious puppy.

'Apparently, she completely stuffed up the final turn. Like, I mean, she practically fell on her butt,' Ava announced smugly.

I didn't mean to, but I felt my jaw drop open. I quickly closed it again.

'And how do you know?' Khalila asked, resting her chin on one hand. With the other, she casually twirled her straw around her cup. I watched as the straw caught on her finger, and a spurt of caramel milk torpedoed through the air. I flinched as it came to land on the sleeve of Ava's white tracksuit jacket.

Ava didn't seem to notice. Instead, she continued talking as if nothing had happened. Meanwhile, the giant caramel milk stain stared back at me. I looked away before she noticed.

'Well, someone, I won't tell you who, was watching the entire audition through the second studio door. They probably saw all your mistakes too, Khalila,' Ava said with a grin, before turning on her heel and marching back to her table. Khalila glared after her.

'*Mamma mia* …What does that mean? Is it true?' I hissed.

Khalila slurped up the final mouthful of milkshake. She narrowed her eyes theatrically as she swallowed. Finally, she spoke. 'I'm not sure.'

I laughed. 'You are more dramatic than any Italian I have ever met. That says a lot.'

Khalila laughed. 'Well, put it this way. Ava talks a lot of rubbish. I can't *really* see Amelia blowing her audition and then being happy about it in the change room. Can you? I reckon Ava's just teasing us. Making us think that maybe we stand a chance as Cinderella, so that we get our hopes up, only to be crushed later.'

I bit my lip. Khalila was probably right. Amelia hadn't stopped practising her turns. There was no way she would have stuffed them up.

'By the way, did you see the milk on Ava's arm?' Khalila said, before dissolving into a fit of laughter.

I raced up the Academy stairs after Khalila, struggling to keep up with her ridiculously long legs. We'd been so busy chatting that we hadn't noticed the rest of the students leave the cafe.

Khalila was fuming. 'I told you Ava was up to no good,' she sputtered. 'Trying to distract us with that stupid story about Amelia falling on her bum, just so she could see the casting list before us!' She was so busy whinging that she didn't notice Amelia coming down the staircase towards us.

'Amelia!' I said loudly, desperate to shut Khalila up. I didn't want Amelia to hear Khalila and think everyone had been gossiping about her. Even though they had. The Academy students were almost as bad as Anna-Maria. *Almost.*

'Are they up?' Khalila asked, gasping for breath. Given the amount of dancing we did each week, you would expect us to be fitter.

Amelia curled her upper lip in disgust at Khalila's lack of athleticism, but nodded.

'And? What did you get?' Khalila asked.

I couldn't tell if Khalila was nervous or excited. She pranced back and forth between steps, as if she didn't know whether she wanted to go upstairs to the Academy or back down and out the door. I turned my attention back to Amelia's face, searching for a sign that things hadn't gone to plan.

Amelia smiled. '*Exactly* the role I wanted,' she said, before pushing past us and heading down the stairs.

'See, told ya,' Khalila said. 'I guess Ava was just messing with us. Well, let's find out what scraps are left for the rest of us, I s'pose.'

I followed slowly behind Khalila. I should've known better than to get my hopes up. Khalila was right, she had warned me. There was no way Miss Lily would give the lead role to someone she barely knew when she had her favourite students. I reminded myself that Amelia deserved the role. Hard work should be rewarded. I was sure I'd enjoy the production no matter what role I'd been given, even if it was in the *corps de ballet* – dancing in a group with the others. Maybe next year I could go for a lead.

'Come on, we will have fun together. The role does not matter,' I said, smiling at Khalila.

'Haha, okay. Whatever you say, Little Miss Sunshine,' Khalila said.

By the time we got to the green room, a crowd had already formed around the noticeboard. We joined the queue and waited patiently. At least, I waited patiently.

Khalila pranced on the spot, craning her neck to try and see over the other students.

Kate and Ava were at the front of the line, giggling and making a fuss. 'Stepsisters!' Ava exclaimed.

'Oh my god, we're gunna have so much fun! We're *practically* sisters already!' Kate said.

Khalila's face contorted in pain. 'That's all we're gunna hear. Every. Single. Lesson,' she said dryly. I laughed, but smiled politely as Ava and Kate walked past.

'Congratulations,' I offered.

The pair exchanged a look. Ava snorted. 'Well, didn't see that one coming,' she said with a grin.

I felt like I was going to vomit. Was the casting really that bad? Finally, we reached the front of the queue. As I took a step towards the noticeboard, I held my breath. '*Ti prego, non un topo,*' I muttered under my breath.

Suddenly, Khalila squealed.

'Vale!'

'*Oh dio*, I am a mouse?' I asked flatly. I couldn't bring myself to look.

'No, you were right. There aren't any mice. Look!' Khalila said. '*You're* Cinderella!'

My stomach did a backflip as I finally forced myself to look at the casting list. 'No … *ma non é possibile,*' I whispered under my breath. But there it was. Printed clearly next to Cinderella, was my name. '*Ma* … Amelia?' I was so shocked I couldn't find any English words.

'She's the Fairy Godmother! God, she must be so angry. Weird, because she didn't seem it,' Khalila said. She scrunched up her nose as she looked back at the list.

The room was spinning. How on earth could I dance Cinderella? I suddenly remembered Khalila and scanned the sheet of paper in search of her name. 'What are you?' I asked.

'Ah … Bird Number Two,' Khalila said flatly.

I couldn't look at her. Just like that, the fun had disappeared. How could I be happy when Khalila had only been given a minor role? I didn't even know there were birds in *Cinderella*. Khalila and I had worked so hard to prepare for the audition and Khalila had helped me a lot. Guilt gnawed at my stomach.

'Hey, don't do that face. I'm fine,' Khalila said with a smile. 'I'm sure the bird dance is cool. I just hope it's not like the birdie dance from kids parties!' she added with a forced smile.

My head spun as I followed Khalila towards the exit. I was Cinderella and I couldn't quite believe it.

9
Amelia

I don't know why I did it, but at that exact moment, it was like something had taken over my brain and I couldn't control the words as they came out of my mouth.

I'd been standing out the front of the Academy, kicking around loose pieces of gravel, angry at the world over the casting. I couldn't believe Miss Lily would give the lead role to someone she barely knew. I had put in so much extra work, stretched my body past its natural limits, not slept in days, and for what? Miss Lily had given the lead role to a stranger and left me with the scraps. No one came to the ballet to watch the stupid Fairy Godmother. They came to see Cinderella. I should have been cast as Cinderella.

I was angry and I was stressed. I kept glancing between the Academy door and the road, willing my mum's car to appear. Inside, I knew everyone would still be huddled around the noticeboard, no doubt laughing at the results. They'd know that me, the favourite, had been given a supporting role. It was mortifying. I wanted to dig a hole and bury myself in it. I needed to get as far away from the Academy as possible. Fast. The last thing I needed was for the other students to come out and rub my face in it. Ava and Kate would be over the moon. At least one of them hadn't landed the lead role. Or perhaps it would have been better if they had. The fact that Miss Lily had given the lead role to a new kid wasn't fair at all. Valentina hadn't done her time.

My audition must have been worse than I thought. I wouldn't have lost the lead over one bad *pirouette*. What if all this time I'd been thinking I was a great dancer, when in actual fact, I was a dud?

I was on the verge of tears and that made me even angrier. I couldn't cry outside the Academy. No one could know how disappointed I was. Imagine if the other kids came out and I was sobbing in the carpark? I'd keel over and die on the spot from humiliation.

When I finally saw Mum's white Suzuki pulling into the carpark, a second wave of panic washed over me. I hadn't even considered what I'd tell Mum. It was one thing for me to be angry at myself, but Mum would be so disappointed. With all the extra private lessons she and Dad were paying for, I should be getting every single lead role. Otherwise, it was just money down the drain. Mum would probably want to dissect the audition – every single step, what went wrong, what I could improve on for next time. Once again, I found myself wishing I had parents that didn't care about ballet. The type of parents that would hear the news and just say something like, *That sucks, honey!* or *Don't be silly! That's a great part to get!*

It was all of those worries put together that led to the worst lie I'd ever told. Maybe even the worse lie *anyone* had ever told.

The minute I got into the car, Mum started. 'So?' She asked.

I couldn't look her in the eye. I was glancing out the window when Ava and Kate emerged from the Academy door, laughing and prancing around excitedly. I wished it were me.

'Hel-lo, Amelia? How'd you go? I've been dying to hear from you,' Mum prodded. She turned the radio down, bracing herself for the news.

That's when it happened. The words flew out of my mouth and as soon as they did, I wished I could pull them back. 'Great! I got the part!'

I don't know why I said it. At first, it wasn't really a lie. I hadn't specified which part I'd got.

'You got Cinderella? I knew it!'

'Mmhmmm.' Then it became a lie. A big, horrible, stupid, idiotic lie.

'I told you hard work pays off. I bet the triple *pirouette* really sealed Lily's decision. You must have blown her socks off with that one.'

'Yeah, I don't think anyone else did a triple.' I wanted to press rewind. Reverse back into the carpark, climb out, then start again, but of course, you can't do that in real life. All I could do was stare out the window, watching the world fly by as my stomach churned angrily.

I spent the entire afternoon trying to figure out how to undo the lie and tell the truth. It's not like I could just say, *Oops, sorry Mum, you know how I just told you I'd been cast as Cinderella? Well, I lied. I actually got one of the smaller roles. That's right, your ballet-obsessed daughter who takes private lessons and has her own home studio wasn't good enough to get the lead.* That would go over like a tonne of bricks.

I didn't know how to fix things and Mum only made it worse by spending the rest of the day celebrating my fake success. We ended up in a Japanese restaurant, my absolute favourite, toasting the lead role.

'I'm so proud of you, honey. Your drive, your determination – you constantly astound me,' Mum said, a glass of champagne held in the air.

'Your mum's right. I was never that disciplined at your age,' Dad said, getting in on the fun.

'You're still not that disciplined,' Mum said with a laugh.

I laughed softly, my eyes glued to my glass of Diet Coke.

'Anyway, to hard work, dedication and the knowledge that it always pays off. Cheers, Amelia,' Mum said, clinking her glass with mine.

Every word of Mum's speech was like a hammer, beating me further and further into the ground. Some people lie all the time and nothing ever comes of it. This wasn't going to be one of those cases. It was the most disastrous, ridiculous lie in the world because eventually the truth would have to come out. I don't know what I'd been thinking. It's not like Mum and Dad would see Valentina performing Cinderella and think it was me. Absolutely nothing good could come of this lie. Nothing.

'You okay, kiddo?' Dad asked, resting his hand on my forearm. 'You look a bit pale.'

'Yeah, it's just …' I paused. I wanted to fess up. I *had* to fess up. Only, I couldn't. I didn't know how. 'I'm just a bit tired.'

'Of course you are, hun,' Mum said. 'You know I always say how proud I am of how hard you work, but you have been burning the candle at both ends lately. It wouldn't hurt you to slow down a bit, you know. Do you think you're doing too much? Dancing too much even?'

I looked at Mum in horror. 'I just had a huge audition. I had to prepare.'

Mum patted my other arm. 'Oh, I know that honey, and I'm not having a go at you. I just worry, that's all.'

'You worry?' I questioned. First I'd heard of it. Unless she meant she was worried about my *arabesque*.

'I worry that you're missing out. You're fourteen. Wouldn't you like to have sleepovers, go to the movies, hang out with your friends a bit on the weekends?'

Mum had clearly lost her mind. She might as well have just announced she was actually part robot. Mum knew better than anyone that if I wanted a career in ballet, sleepovers, movie dates and all the other normal teenage activities weren't a part of life. How could I go to a sleepover, stay up all night talking and eating sugar and then expect to have enough energy to dance the next day?

'You didn't do those things either,' I reminded her.

'I know. And maybe sometimes I wish I had,' Mum said quietly.

I couldn't believe what I was hearing. I studied Mum's face closely. Her eyes looked so sad. It was almost as if she regretted ever becoming a professional dancer. 'I'm fine,' I said, rushing to lift the mood. 'Honest. I love ballet and wouldn't change a thing.' Except for maybe the part where I'd lied about being Cinderella. I took a sip of my drink, my eyes still fixed on Mum. Was I missing out by not going to the movies or to sleepovers? Who would I even go with? I'd turned down so many invites from the kids at school because of dance classes, that no one even bothered to invite me anymore. As for the Academy, without Alice there wasn't really anyone I wanted to spend time with. An image of Valentina and Khalila laughing together popped into my mind. I quickly pushed it away.

'Okay, we have unagi, yakitori and the world's best sashimi,' the waitress said, cutting through the tension.

'Ah, unagi!' Dad said. He held his fingers up to the side of his head, impersonating an old episode of the TV show *Friends* where Ross thought unagi meant to be in a total state of awareness.

'Salmon skin roll,' I said, joining in with the voice of Rachel, my favourite character. Dad and I burst out laughing. It was exactly what I needed. I was obsessed with *Friends*. The waitress smiled and shook her head. Somehow, I don't think we were the first ones to make the joke.

'You two,' Mum said with a soft chuckle.

Sometimes, I think she gets a bit jealous of Dad and me. We have a special bond. If I need ballet advice, I'll go to Mum – well sometimes – but anything else, it's Dad. He's just so much less intense than Mum is and with the Academy already being such a high-pressure environment, that's usually what I need.

'Hey, isn't that one of your dance friends?' Mum said, glancing towards the door.

My head whipped around to see Ava and her family making their way into the restaurant. I felt my entire body tense up. There was no way Ava could talk to Mum. She'd blow my cover for sure. I had to stop her coming over. Only, Mum was already standing up, waving Ava's family over.

'Mum, Mum, what are you doing?' I hissed.

'What do you mean what am I doing? I'm saying hello. I think I've met her parents before.'

'Mum, that's Ava. I don't like …' I trailed off as Ava and her family reached our table.

'Amelia, nice to see you,' Ava said chirpily. She could be so fake sometimes.

'Hi, love!' Mum said to Ava, before turning to her parents. 'Sorry, I'm Liana. Liana Scott. I think we've met before? This is my husband, Rob.' Mum shook hands with Ava's parents. 'We're celebrating today's casting. Ava, honey, how did you go?'

'Celebrating, huh?' Ava said, giving me a funny look. My stomach spun faster than a washing machine on the spin cycle. 'We're doing the same. I'm one of the Stepsisters.'

Ava becomes a completely different person when she talks to adults. Her voice goes all high and she becomes sickly sweet.

'That's fantastic, congratulations!' Mum said. 'Celebrations all round. We're just so proud of Amelia.'

I swallowed hard, praying Mum would stop talking. Of course, she didn't.

'These girls just work so hard, don't they? Honestly, the things they do in class now … the talent, it all just blows me away. The expectations are so much higher than they were when I was a teenager at the Academy,' Mum said.

'Miss Lily definitely pushes us. Surprise casting though, wasn't it?' Ava said.

Mum looked confused, but then smiled sympathetically. 'You all work so hard, it must be difficult for her to choose.'

Judging by Mum's response, she obviously thought Ava was bitter about me getting the lead. If only. I was grateful when Mum turned to Ava's parents and began making small talk.

'So, you're celebrating?' Ava asked, her eyebrow raised.

'Yep.'

'That's surprising. I thought you'd be miserable,' Ava said.

A fake smile was frozen on my face. I glanced at Mum out of the corner of my eye, checking to see whether she'd heard Ava's comment. Thankfully, she and Dad were deep in conversation.

'Not at all. It's a fabulous role,' I said. I had to be careful what I said. I didn't want Ava knowing my true thoughts about the casting.

'Maybe. But seriously, what was Miss Lily thinking? It makes no sense. I thought you'd feel the same. So much for loyalty to your students,' Ava said, crossing her arms.

I felt the exact same way, but there was no way I'd let Ava know that. 'It is what it is,' I said. It was a classic Mum response, the line she always used when she didn't want to give her opinion on a heated topic.

Ava studied my face. I didn't let my smile drop. 'Well, I guess we'll just have to wait and see how rehearsals go then,' she said.

'Guess so,' I said, waving her off as her parents said goodbye and headed over to their table.

My breath slowed as soon as she was gone. That had been close. As much as I wanted to undo my lie, I didn't want anyone else around when I did.

10
Valentina

'*Evviva! Cenerentola!*' Caterina yelled, prancing around the kitchen. 'Hooray! Cinderella!'

'Cate, stop saying that,' Giuseppe groaned.

I didn't blame him. Since telling my family the news about casting, Caterina had been jumping around the house nonstop, yelling that at the top of her voice. I'd been home for a good two hours, so the novelty was starting to wear off for everyone.

'It's my favourite fairytale. Isn't it yours too, Vale?' Caterina said. She grabbed my hands and danced around me.

I laughed. 'Yes, I suppose so.'

Caterina was by far the most excited of the whole family. Everyone was happy for me, but they didn't really understand how big a deal it was. They all acted like me being cast as Cinderella was a given and nothing to be surprised about.

'Of course you did!' Anna-Maria had responded when I told her, kissing me once on each cheek. Not surprisingly, she and the boys were at our house when I shared the news. 'Italians are the best at ballet!'

I appreciated her faith in my dancing, but I wished she'd stop saying that. I wanted her to know the audition hadn't been easy, that I had been up against a whole class of extremely talented dancers. Like Amelia. I still couldn't believe she hadn't been given the lead. I just hoped she didn't hate me for getting it.

The minute Mamma heard the news, she wrapped me up in one of her giant bear hugs and planted a trillion kisses on my forehead. 'Didn't I tell you Australia would be full of opportunities?' she said. 'We need to celebrate. I'll make your favourite dinner. We can even have tiramisu for dessert.'

'Is Papà working tonight?' I asked. Papà had been working really long hours at the restaurant lately. I felt like I'd barely seen him.

'*Sì*. It's Saturday. The busiest night of the week, *cara mia*. But we can still celebrate. Papà can eat his serve when he gets home. Now tell me, were the other dancers happy that you got the part? They must think you are very talented.'

'Khalila was very excited, but she always seems to be excited. I'm not sure yet about the others. They were too busy talking about what roles they had been given. I hope they aren't mad at me.'

'Mad? Why would they be mad? Are they not nice to

you?' Mamma's face filled with concern.

'I always heard ballerinas were nasty,' Anna-Maria piped up. Sometimes I wished she and her boys weren't always at our house. It would be nice to just have some family time. Like, *actual* family time. Not my family and every other family in the street that was somewhat related to us.

'No, they aren't nasty. That's not what I meant. I'm just new, that's all. There's another girl, Amelia, everyone thought she would get to play Cinderella. She's the hardest working dancer I've ever met. Like, she never stops dancing. Khalila thinks she lives at the Academy. Which is just silly, but *that's* how often she's there. I bet she's mad that I got the part instead of her,' I said.

'Ah, the jealousy. You can't help it if you're more talented.' Anna-Maria said with a shrug.

With my back turned to Anna-Maria, I rolled my eyes, making a face only Mamma could see. I saw her eyes twinkle, but she withheld her smile. Anna-Maria annoyed her too sometimes.

'*Bella mia*, you can't always worry about everyone else. Work hard like we've taught you, be kind and that's all you can do,' Mamma said. She tossed a tablecloth at me. 'Now you can practise being Cinderella by setting the table.'

I caught the tablecloth and laughed. 'How many of us are there? Salvatore?'

'He's out,' Mamma said.

'Again? Where?' I asked.

Mamma just shrugged. As long as he came home each night, she didn't ask questions. I felt like I'd barely seen Salvatore since we'd moved to Australia.

'Anna-Maria, are you staying for dinner too?' I asked. I hoped the answer would be no, but I had a feeling it wouldn't be.

'Is Pope Francesco Catholic?' She asked.

I sighed and set extra places at the table for Anna-Maria and her boys.

The following morning, I found Papà at the kitchen table, hunched over an exercise book. He'd returned home from the restaurant ridiculously late and I was surprised to see him awake so early.

'The cat … sat … on the … mat,' he said, slowly pronouncing the English words, before immediately growling in Italian, 'Who cares if the cat is sitting on a mat?'

'How's your English going?' I asked, planting a kiss on his cheek.

'It's useless,' he said. 'These phrases won't help me at the restaurant.'

'You never know. If there's a cat sitting on a mat at the

restaurant, that's a pretty big problem and you should tell someone,' I said with a grin.

Papà laughed and pinched my cheek. 'Cheeky girl,' he said.

He was right. It was a stupid phrase. Papà didn't really need to speak English working at the restaurant anyway, given the kitchen was mostly full of other Italians. He needed phrases that would help him *outside* of the restaurant. He hated that Mamma had to deal with everything, like banking, schooling and shopping.

'Help me with this one, my clever ballerina,' he said, pointing at the book.

I leant in over his shoulder to help, just as Nonna came shuffling into the kitchen. 'What are you doing?' she asked.

'Learning English. Maybe you could help us,' I said cheekily.

Nonna shook her head and flicked her hand in my direction. 'I'll teach you about things that actually matter,' she muttered in fast dialect. She handed me a bag full of beans she'd picked from the garden. 'Do something useful. Peel these beans while you're standing there. I need them for lunch.'

'You shouldn't be wasting your time helping me anyway,' Papà said. 'You've been dancing so much, you must have a lot of homework to do.'

'Later,' I said. I opened the bag and began removing beans from their pods.

'Later? It's always *later* when I ask you or your brother about your studies. You both forget why we moved here,' Papà said, shaking his head. 'You're too busy dancing.'

It was the first time I'd heard him speak negatively about my dancing. 'My grades are good. Don't worry, I will study today. I can dance and study. Probably even at the same time,' I winked, trying to lighten the mood.

Caterina came skipping into the kitchen, shouting Cinderella at the top of her lungs. Abandoning his own studies, Papà jumped up and scooped her into the air. He flipped her upside down, holding her by the ankles.

She giggled hysterically. '*Aiuto, aiuto!*' she cried.

'Sorry, I don't speak Italian,' I said to her.

'Vale ... Help, help!' she yelled.

Smiling, I wrestled her from Papà's grip. Safely in my arms, she stuck her tongue out at Papà.

'Why were you yelling Cinderella?' he asked. I thought Mamma might have told him the news.

'Because Vale is Cinderella. She was the best dancer, Papà,' Caterina announced proudly.

'I had my audition yesterday,' I explained. 'I got the lead role in the ballet performance.'

Papà smiled. His eyes looked so tired, but still, they

twinkled. 'My ballerina, always the best,' he planted a kiss on my forehead, then one on Caterina's. 'But remember, we came here for a better future. You can dance all you like, but you need to study and do well at school.'

'Of course,' I said. The pressure was on.

'What should I cook for dinner tomorrow night? Giovanni di Angelo and his family are coming to see us.'

'Tomorrow night? I won't be here. I have my first *Cinderella* rehearsal.'

'But we haven't seen the di Angelo's since we moved here. You have to be home. You can go to rehearsal the following night,' Papà said.

So much for dancing as much as I liked.

'It doesn't work like that. I can't miss a rehearsal,' I said. My voice was getting higher and higher as panic rose in my chest. The Southern Italians value three things above all else: family, food and tradition. Me going to a ballet rehearsal instead of having dinner with the family, went against all three.

'But the di Angelo's will expect to see you. What will they think when I say you are out dancing?' Papà said, his voice raising.

'Papà, don't yell,' I said. He had a bad habit of raising his voice the minute he got stressed.

'I'm not yelling,' he said, still yelling.

Mamma walked into the room. 'What's happened?' she asked, looking between my worried face and Papà's.

'The di Angelo's are coming for dinner tomorrow night and I have ballet rehearsal,' I explained.

'She can't go. She must be here,' Papà said.

'Papà ...' I pleaded.

'She can't miss her rehearsal. She can see the di Angelo's another time,' Mamma said. She walked across to the stove and began preparing a pot of coffee.

'They will think she's disrespectful,' Papà said, shaking his head.

'When they hear she is the star of the show, they will understand. We will invite them to the performance,' Mamma said, spooning ground coffee into the pot.

Thank goodness for Mamma. I only hoped no other family events would clash with rehearsals. I'd got my way once, but I didn't see it happening again.

11
Amelia

It had been a long, torturous weekend, celebrating a lie that seemed to be growing bigger and bigger by the minute. The icing on the cake had been when Mum insisted that we watch an old recording of her dancing as Cinderella. It made me want to throw up.

In the brief moments I had to myself, I googled videos of famous ballerinas dancing as the Fairy Godmother. I'll admit, they were all wonderful. There was actually nothing wrong with the role, and if I hadn't been so shocked when I found out, I might have actually been excited about it. From what I'd seen, the Fairy Godmother was a real show stopper. It wasn't the lead, but it was pretty close.

By the time Monday came around, I was ready to come clean to Mum and Dad and accept the role I'd been given. There was just one thing I had to do first. I had to speak to Miss Lily to make sure there hadn't been a mistake. If I was going to fess up to my lie, I had to be certain that dancing Cinderella was 100 percent off the cards.

Class didn't start until five pm, so I got to the Academy an hour early so I could speak to Miss Lily without anyone else listening in. I found her in the costume room. Her slender frame was bent over a box, rifling through its contents. She was so preoccupied, she didn't hear me come in.

'Um, Miss Lily?'

She still didn't hear me. Instead, she pulled a yellow tutu out of a box and tossed it over her head. I ducked as it flew towards me.

'Miss Lily?' I tried again. Still nothing. 'Miss Lily!' I yelled.

That got her attention. She jumped and looked over her shoulder. 'Amelia! You scared the life out of me. I didn't see you there.' She continued to sift through the costumes. 'I know it's in here somewhere …' she said.

'What are you looking for?' I couldn't help myself. The costume room was bursting at the seams with tutus, gowns, wings – every costume you could imagine and more. As kids, Alice and I would sometimes sneak into the costume closet and play dress-ups. One time, Miss Lily caught us. We were both dressed up in ball gowns that were miles too big, with tiaras on our heads. We could tell Miss Lily wanted to laugh, but she had to make a point of telling us off for sneaking into a room we weren't supposed to be in. Our punishment was mirror duty. We had to clean all of the studio mirrors. Given our height at the time, we didn't do a very good job. The thought made me smile. I missed Alice.

'If my dusty old memory doesn't fail me, Cinderella's dress is in here somewhere,' Miss Lily said, tossing more tutus out of a box. 'I haven't the foggiest idea where though. Honestly, this closet's out of control. I've been saying for years that it needs a good tidy-up. There are never enough hours in a day.'

'Maybe I could help you tidy it up some time?' I offered.

'You're an angel, I'll hold you to that,' Miss Lily said, still rummaging through boxes.

It was now or never. 'I was hoping I could have a quick chat to you,' I said nervously.

Miss Lily's eyes darted around the room, before falling on a plastic crate at the far side of the room. 'Hmm … maybe I put it in there,' she said, stepping over discarded tutus to make her way over to the box. 'Can you put those away, please?' she said, waving her hand at the tutus.

I began picking up the tutus, carefully stacking them upside down on top of one another. It was even harder to talk to Miss Lily than I'd expected. Perhaps I'd picked the wrong time.

Miss Lily lifted the crate down from its shelf. She paused for a moment and studied my face over the top of her glasses. Her thin lips puckered together in thought. 'What did you say you wanted to talk about?'

'It's about *Cinderella*,' I began. I knew I had to tread really carefully. I didn't want to sound ungrateful, or like a brat.

'What about *Cinderella*? Aha! Here it is!' Miss Lily said, pulling a brown dress out of the crate. 'A bit dusty, but I think it'll still work.'

'Well, I know we're not supposed to question casting, but well …' my heart was thumping so loudly, I wouldn't be surprised if Miss Lily could hear it.

'Amelia, my decision is final. Dancing the Fairy Godmother is nothing to be sneezed at,' Miss Lily said, folding the dress over her arm, before replacing the crate on the shelf.

'I know. But, I just want to know what I did wrong. Was it the triple turn?' I clutched the tutus against my body, shielding myself from Miss Lily's answer.

'You're right, you made a terrible mess of your *pirouette* and it was only because you were indecisive. As I always say, you need to commit to the number of *pirouettes* you're going to do, *before* you start turning – otherwise you'll either have too much, or not enough momentum. Neither will work properly,' Miss Lily said.

I knew it. If only I'd played it safe and stuck to a double turn.

'But Amelia, it's not the *pirouette* that stopped you from being cast as Cinderella,' Miss Lily said, pushing her way past the costume racks towards me.

'It wasn't?' I could've sworn the rest of my dance had been flawless.

'No, your audition was beautiful, but this time, Valentina was better for the part. It's hard to hear, but sometimes you've just got to accept that someone else will come to an audition and be better suited to the role than you,' Miss Lily said. 'It doesn't mean you did anything wrong, or that you didn't try your hardest, it just means someone else stood out. When Valentina danced that audition, she danced it with heart and it was beautiful.'

If Miss Lily had said I'd blown the audition because of my *pirouette*, I might have survived, but her actual reason was enough to destroy me. To dance without heart is to dance without life. I was a complete disaster. 'Okay. Thanks for letting me know,' I said quietly. My voice was no more than a whisper. I was trying to act mature, but I felt my lip quiver as I spoke.

'Amelia, aside from the *pirouette*, your audition really was beautiful. That's why you were cast as the Fairy Godmother. I need two powerful leading ladies,' Miss Lily said, patting my arm as she walked towards the door.

I sighed. So according to Miss Lily, I had been given a

lead role, just not the one I wanted. Maybe, just maybe though, she would see me dancing beside Valentina and realise she'd made a mistake. Maybe she'd switch us. It was a long shot, but a shot nonetheless. Maybe it wasn't worth coming clean to Mum and Dad yet. There might still be a chance of me dancing Cinderella after all.

Twenty minutes into the first rehearsal and my chances of playing Cinderella were looking better than I'd thought. The choreography was hard and Miss Lily expected us to pick things up quickly. Valentina was a hot mess. For someone who was usually so precise with her movements, she was all over the place. She struggled to keep up with the steps and it was as if she was no longer capable of dancing on pointe. As much as I felt sorry for her, every mistake she made took me one step closer to dancing as Cinderella. The way she was going, Miss Lily would be begging me to take over as the lead in no time.

We were learning one of the early scenes of the production, the one where the invitation for the Grand Ball arrives at Cinderella's house. There were only four characters needed for the scene – Cinderella, the two Stepsisters and the Evil Stepmother – but the studio was still full. Miss Lily had a rule that even if you weren't in a scene, you still had to attend the rehearsal, stand at the back and learn one of the roles. Apparently, it was to keep our minds and bodies working, but I think it was also Miss Lily's backup plan in case someone got sick the week of the performance.

Naturally, I was learning the role of Cinderella. I had to admit, the choreography was hard and there was a lot to remember. I watched closely as Miss Lily demonstrated, memorising the tiny details that would make the dance come to life. As I danced behind Valentina, I did my best to make the steps look easy and effortless, just like a true professional would. It was something I always found impressive whenever I was watching one of the big companies perform. Being a dancer myself, I knew just how hard their steps were, yet they always made them look so easy. In my opinion, that's the difference between an amateur dancer and a professional, and put it this way, Vale didn't look at all like a professional today. If she wasn't forgetting the choreography, she was stumbling out of it, and deep down inside, I couldn't have been happier.

Most of the other kids were just stuffing around at the back of the room. They pretended to learn the steps whenever Miss Lily was looking, but they spent the majority of the time chatting or practising their turns and jumps. If I wanted to impress Miss Lily and show her that I was the better Cinderella, I had to do everything properly. I pushed myself as hard as I had for the audition. I could feel even more blisters taking up residence on my toes, but I ignored them. It was nothing that couldn't be fixed with a Band-Aid later.

I stood diagonally behind Valentina, shadowing her every move. If the music was playing, I was performing. I could feel Valentina's eyes glued to my reflection in the mirror, copying my every move. I ignored her, holding my head high as I made the performance look like a breeze.

'Come on, Valentina, keep up with the music. You're supposed to be floating through the movements. I want you to work hard, but I don't want to see the effort,' Miss Lily yelled over the music. 'Amelia, that's beautiful, but you can back off a bit. Save your energy for your rehearsal.'

Instead of backing off, I ramped up my energy even further. I was being noticed and I loved it. Out of the corner of my eye I saw Valentina stumble.

Miss Lily paused the music. 'Come on, Valentina, I'm seeing too many little mistakes. From the top please.'

I took a step back, discreetly trying to catch my breath. It was the third time Miss Lily had stopped the music in the past five minutes. If Valentina kept this up, it would take a whole year to get the show ready. As I held up my arms, ready to begin, I stole a glance at her in the mirror.

Her eyes looked glassy, like she was on the verge of tears. It was only the first rehearsal. If she wanted to cry now, how was she going to cope closer to performance time when the pressure really increased?

'If she doesn't get it right soon, we'll never make it onto the stage,' I heard Ava whisper to Kate. The pair were leaning against the ballet barre, waiting for their turn to dance. It was taking so long to get through Cinderella's solo, that the Stepsisters hadn't even made it into the scene yet.

Kate rolled her eyes. 'I don't know why we even came today,' she responded.

Miss Lily started the music. I flashed my stage smile and began to perform. Less than thirty seconds in, Valentina stumbled out of an *arabesque*. Miss Lily stopped the music.

I came to a sudden halt, digging my fists into my hips in frustration. It was getting ridiculous. We were wasting so much time.

'*Mi dispiace* … I am sorry. I do not know what is wrong with me,' Vale murmured.

'I think you need a break. Go get a drink, then go over the parts you don't know. I want to work with Ava, Kate and Sarah for a bit,' Miss Lily said.

''bout time,' Kate muttered, as she pushed herself off the barre and made her way towards the centre of the room.

Valentina's shoulders slumped as she walked over to her drink bottle.

I grabbed my own bottle and took a small sip, watching Valentina out of the corner of my eye. I did feel a bit sorry for her. I didn't enjoy seeing someone else struggle, particularly someone who was trying so hard, but this was war. If I wanted the lead role, Valentina had to go.

Vale leant back against the barre and rested her head against the brick wall behind it. She closed her eyes and sighed heavily.

My natural instinct was to tell her to hang in there, but I bit my tongue. I was just about to go back and practise, when Valentina spoke.

'You make it look very easy,' she said, her eyes still closed.

'I'm used to Miss Lily's choreography,' I said with a shrug. What I actually wanted to say was, *this role was made for me.*

'*Beata te,*' Valentina said glumly.

I raised my eyebrows questioningly.

'You are lucky. I guess I will just have to work harder.'

'Well, if you want to be the lead, yeah,' I replied. I placed my water bottle back in my pigeonhole with a thud, before walking away.

The first shots had been fired. I didn't say it to be mean, I said it as a warning. If you're the lead performer you had to be prepared to put in more work than anyone else. If Valentina wasn't prepared to do that, I was.

12
Valentina

A good artist never blames their tools, so I couldn't tell Miss Lily or Amelia that the reason I couldn't keep up in rehearsal was because my pointe shoes were *morte* – dead.

When pointe shoes die, they get so soft that they no longer offer enough support to dance. My shoes were softer than slippers. Dancing on your toes isn't the most natural thing in the world and it only works if you've got the right shoes holding all of your bones, joints, ligaments and tendons in the right place. When your shoes start to get old and soft, everything falls out of place and dancing on pointe becomes not only impossible, but also dangerous.

For the entire rehearsal, my muscles strained to hold me in place, but there was only so much they could do. Inside I was screaming at myself to take my shoes off, to say something before I caused any damage, but my pride wouldn't let me. Instead, I pushed harder and harder. With so much panic pulsing through me, I couldn't understand Miss Lily's corrections, but it was clear she was annoyed.

And I didn't blame her. I was a mess. One rehearsal in and she was probably wondering why she'd chosen me in the first place.

Having Amelia at rehearsal was making everything a million times worse. She was 100 percent made for the role and she was out-shining me every time the music played. Even when it wasn't playing. While I was hunched at the side of the studio, gasping for breath, Amelia looked like she was ready to model for a dance magazine. It wasn't fair. The other kids weren't bothering to learn the extra roles like Amelia was. Plus, she could have chosen to shadow the Stepsisters, or the Evil Stepmother, but no, of course she had to learn the lead. I felt like she was on my heels, threatening to take my spot as Cinderella the entire time. The worst part? When Amelia danced, it was impossible not to watch.

In the middle of the studio, the Stepsisters were learning their choreography. One of them was pretending to play the piano, while the other danced clumsily alongside her. I couldn't help but laugh as Ava pretended to wobble in her pointe shoes. She looked like Bambi, unable to control her limbs. She and Kate were having the time of their lives. Part of me wished it was me and Khalila. Even if we didn't look a thing alike.

I reluctantly made my way over to the back corner where Amelia was going over the routine. *My routine.* I watched for a second, then joined in midway through the sequence. I studied Amelia closely, doing my best to learn the steps. She sashayed through them like she barely had to think at all. I struggled to keep up in my old shoes. A million swear words flew through my mind –words that would probably send Nonna into cardiac arrest. I'd never dare say them aloud, but at that moment, I was in so much pain that they had taken over my brain. I was so busy watching Amelia in the reflection of the mirror, that I wasn't prepared for her to stop suddenly. I slammed straight into the back of her.

'Umph! *Mannaggia!*'

Amelia rubbed her back dramatically. 'It's really not your day. Is it?' she said dryly.

'Eh, no,' I muttered. I waited for Amelia to start going over the choreography again, but instead, she began working on her *pirouettes*. Obviously, she didn't need to practise anymore. *Beata lei!*

I took a deep breath and started again. I was in complete agony. My feet and legs protested against the movements. I came down off my toes and instead began marking the steps on *demi-pointe*. I needed to save my shoes for the moments when Miss Lily was actually watching.

I glanced at the clock. There were still twenty minutes left of rehearsal. Twenty minutes seemed like an eternity. Especially because my mind had gone completely blank.

I'd been so focused on my sore feet that I couldn't for the life of me remember what I was supposed to be doing. I glanced over at Amelia, she was focused and about to push off into a *pirouette*.

'Um, Amelia?' I interrupted nervously.

She sighed impatiently and straightened herself up. 'Yes?'

'You know in the dance when I do two little *changement* jumps, then the little turn on the spot?'

'You mean a *soutenu*?'

'*Si*, a *soutenu*. Erm ... what comes next?' I asked. I felt like an absolute idiot having to ask Amelia for help when it was my dance, not hers.

Amelia obviously felt the same. She looked disgusted. 'You *relevé* into an *arabesque*,' she said, turning back to the mirror.

I nodded and tried the sequence again. I reached my leg up past ninety degrees into an *arabesque*, before gently lowering it back to the ground. A strand of hair had fallen in front of my eyes. I puffed out of the corner of my lips, trying to move it.

The sight of Amelia performing three perfect *pirouettes* caught my eye. Ava must have been lying when she said Amelia had stuffed up her turns in the audition. They looked pretty good to me. But, if she had done them perfectly, then why hadn't she been given the lead role? It made no sense.

I shook my head to bring my focus back to my own rehearsal. I danced easily, up until the *arabesque*, before things began to go downhill once again. I glanced over at Amelia, daring myself to ask for help. She was more intimidating than an angry Anna-Maria.

'Um, Amelia?'

As if she hadn't heard, Amelia kept turning.

I tried again. 'Um, Amelia? You know that part with the *piqué* turns, how many are there?'

Amelia planted her foot onto the ground and spun around to face me.

'Valentina, not to be rude, but it's not my job to teach you *your* choreography,' she spat out the words as if they were poison, before marching to the other side of the room.

I winced. I was on my own now. How could I impress Miss Lily with dead pointe shoes and a rotten memory? I didn't stand a chance. On the other side of the room, Amelia had positioned herself next to Miss Lily, smiling and offering to help with the Stepsisters' dance. I could barely look at her.

When rehearsal finally finished, I decided to hang back in the studio. I was beyond embarrassed. I knew Miss

Lily was probably regretting giving me the lead and I was determined to change her mind. Alone in the studio, there was no pressure. I kicked off my dead pointe shoes and prepared to master the dance.

As I glided across the room, my heart floated back to my old studio in Italy. I pictured the small space and the way the light streamed through the high windows, bouncing off the mirrors. I could practically smell Maestra Anna's floral perfume – the one everyone hated because it was too strong and tickled our nostrils whenever she came near. Thinking of my old studio, without my shoes and without Amelia, everything felt right, like it was supposed to. I only wished I could've danced like that in rehearsal, when it actually mattered.

When I could no longer ignore the angry twitch of my muscles, I knew it was time to stop. I sat down on the studio floor and massaged the arches of my feet. My feet looked terrible. There were at least three new blisters and my arches were throbbing.

'Here you are!' Khalila said, swinging around the doorframe.

'Here I am,' I said with a smile. I wished Khalila had been in today's rehearsal. Having a friendly face there might have helped. Instead, she had been in the other studio, learning one of the bird dances.

'How'd you go, Cindy?' Khalila said, plonking herself down on the floor. She opened her legs out to the side and pushed herself into the middle splits, before leaning forward to lay her stomach on the ground. She made it look like the most comfortable position in the world.

'Like a disaster,' I said. I continued to massage one of my feet, slowly moving down the ball of my foot to my toes. 'My pointe shoes are *morte* ... dead... and I could not dance. Amelia looked like a shining star.'

'Uff, that's rough,' Khalila said. She rested her chin on her hands and looked thoughtfully up at me. 'Did you tell Miss Lily about your shoes?'

'No. It would have sounded like an excuse. Especially next to Amelia. I looked like I had never danced in my life. I could not remember a thing. I asked Amelia for help and she might as well have spat in my eye,' I said glumly. I lay back onto the wooden studio floor and glanced up at the ceiling. My eyes felt so heavy that I wondered if I could close them, just for a moment.

Khalila laughed. 'You did what? Geez, you're brave! What did you expect?' she asked. She effortlessly closed her legs behind her so she was lying flat on her stomach and propped herself up on her elbows.

'What?' I asked.

'Well, you're Cindy ... Cinderella, her dream role. Asking

her for help is a bit of a slap in the face. Or a spit in the eye, as you say,' Khalila said with a laugh.

I hadn't thought of it like that. In my family and even at my old school, everyone helped everyone. If anything, we were probably too helpful. I usually felt honoured if someone wanted my help with ballet, but I guess that'd be different if they had the role I wanted.

'I mean, if you think about it, it's like Miss Lily said she wasn't good enough for the role, yet she's actually doing it better than you are at the moment,' Khalila said.

'You are not helping.'

'Sorry, I didn't mean it like that,' Khalila said. 'Don't stress. It's only day one of rehearsals. Get some new shoes and some sleep and you'll nail it. Miss Lily picked you for a reason, remember?'

'*Grazie.* How was bird rehearsal? Can you fly yet?'

Khalila's laugh tinkled in my ears. 'Actually, it was awesome! We're like the mice, only cooler. We're the ones that get you ready for the ball. No flying, unless you count some huge jumps, but the costume sounds like it's gunna be epic!' Khalila said.

'Epic?' It was one of Khalila's favourite words and I had no idea what it meant. I assumed it meant cool, but I'd been wrong before.

'Out-of-this-world incredible,' Khalila explained.

I was just about to say I wished I were a bird, when I realised, Khalila probably would have preferred to be Cinderella, too. I bit my lip and squeezed until the pain felt worse than today's rehearsal had.

I put up with my dead shoes for the entire week. It was torture and by the end of it, my feet were absolutely killing me and the entire class thought I was a terrible dancer. At least that's how it felt.

On Sunday, I finally mustered up the courage to ask Papà for new pointe shoes. Money had been tight since the move and I hated asking, but I couldn't go another day in my old shoes. Papà sighed at the request, pointe shoes were expensive, but as I knew he would, he reached straight for his wallet and pulled out a wad of cash. As well as being incredibly stubborn, he was also incredibly proud. There was no way he would have his daughter dancing in old, broken shoes.

I was determined to start the new week off well and prove to everyone that I was actually a half-decent dancer. It's a shame the universe had other plans. Mamma's driver's licence was taking forever to sort out, so whenever Papà was at work, Anna-Maria was my chauffeur. I was grateful, but aside from her rally-car driving, there was one big problem.

Anna-Maria ran on Italian time, which was very different to actual time. She didn't understand the importance of punctuality, meaning we were always running late. So far, I'd managed to get to all of my ballet classes on time by telling her they started half an hour before schedule.

On Monday afternoon, that didn't go to plan. We had to detour past the dance store to get my new shoes, but that wasn't even the reason we were running late. As I sat in the front of Anna-Maria's car, frantically sewing ribbons onto my new shoes, we suddenly veered off course.

'Wait, where are we going?' I asked, knowing full well it wasn't to the Academy. I stared helplessly out the window, questioning how much damage I'd cause if I jumped out of a moving car.

'I need to stop at the butcher's,' she said. 'It won't take long. Why are you panicked? We have plenty of time.'

That might have been true if anyone else was detouring past the butcher. Not Anna-Maria. The butcher was, of course, a friend of Anna-Maria's. Twenty minutes after she left me waiting in the car, I had finished sewing my shoes and was still waiting for her to re-emerge. I glanced at my watch. My heart rate was increasing with every minute she was gone. Rehearsal was due to start at five pm. That was only fifteen minutes away. I was running out of time to get changed and warm up.

With no sign of Anna-Maria, I grabbed my dance bag from the back seat and began awkwardly wiggling into my ballet tights. I pulled them up beneath my school dress, then after checking no one was around, quickly began pulling my leotard up too.

By the time Anna-Maria re-emerged, I was completely dressed for ballet, hair in a bun and all. Rehearsal had already started.

'You got changed in the car?' Anna-Maria asked, mortified. '*Mamma mia,* what if someone had seen you?'

'I'm running late. No one saw, don't worry.'

'We aren't late,' she said. She slammed her foot on the accelerator and reversed out of the car bay without even checking the rear-view mirror. My heart launched into my throat.

'Rehearsal started five minutes ago,' I said. I tried to keep my voice calm, but I was on the verge of a panic attack.

'What's five minutes?' Anna-Maria said, waving her hand in the air.

That's the problem when someone runs on Italian time. Five minutes, ten minutes, it's all completely irrelevant so long as they arrive eventually. *Eventually* didn't really cut it at a prestigious ballet school.

I barged through the studio door fifteen minutes into the rehearsal. The music was playing and I looked around to take in what was going on. My jaw dropped. Amelia was dancing as Cinderella. Khalila looked over at me and held her hands up questioningly. I just shook my head. What could I say?

When the music stopped, Miss Lily turned to face me. 'Valentina, rehearsal started at five pm. Sharp. I do not tolerate tardiness.'

'*Mi dispiace* … I am so sorry,' I said.

'Let this be a warning. Do not let it happen again,' Miss Lily said firmly. 'Amelia, thank you so much for stepping in so I could work out that sequence of steps. You can return to your own role now.'

Amelia nodded politely at Miss Lily, but glared at me as she made her way back across the room. If I thought the pressure had been high before, it was now through the roof. I couldn't give anyone any more reasons to question my lead role.

In today's scene, the Fairy Godmother was getting Cinderella ready for the Grand Ball with the help of her magical birds – one of them was Khalila.

'Now I've already started teaching the choreography and I do not want to waste time. Valentina, I hope your brain is switched on,' Miss Lily said. I swallowed nervously. 'The birds have already learnt most of their choreography, so it's a matter of slotting you and Amelia in.'

Khalila pinched my elbow to get my attention. 'You just wait. It's amazing!'

I smiled. Her positive energy was contagious. I couldn't afford for Miss Lily to see us talking though. I didn't want her to think I wasn't taking things seriously. As we went through the choreography, I kept a close watch on Miss Lily's face. I was trying to gauge whether she was happy with me or not. It was tough to tell, her face was impossible to read. Kind of like Papà's during a Briscola tournament. Behind her glasses, her eyes darted back and forth between dancers, her lips taut with concentration.

My new shoes felt stiff against my feet. I once again cursed Anna-Maria for making me late. My shoes would take time to break in and I should have warmed up more in them before class. My toes felt like sardines, squashed together in a can.

When Miss Lily's critique finally came, it shot out faster than the bullets of a gun.

'Khalila! Extend your arms, they look like dead trees. Liam – I asked for soft smiles, you're not the Cheshire cat, Mya – sloppy fingers!' she yelled over the music. Her voice blended in with the music and without being able to concentrate on each word, all I could do was listen out for my name.

'Very good, Valentina. It's coming together well,' Miss Lily said, after we'd run the scene through a couple of times.

I breathed a sigh of relief. It was a million times easier to dance when I didn't have Amelia shadowing my every move.

'Amelia, you know the steps, but I need to see you telling the story when you dance now,' Miss Lily said.

Amelia had her hands on her hips, trying to catch her breath. 'Sorry?' she questioned.

'You're going through the motions. Your technique is good, I'm not concerned about that,' Miss Lily explained. 'But stop looking at yourself in the mirror and don't forget, the Fairy Godmother *cares* about Cinderella. She's about to make her dreams come true. I need you to show me that.'

I studied Amelia's face throughout Miss Lily's speech. There was a fire behind her eyes. Despite her cool exterior, she wasn't happy. When Miss Lily finished, Amelia nodded swiftly, before making her way back to her starting position.

'The Fairy Godmother *cares* about Cinderella. This ought to be good,' Khalila muttered as she walked past me. She grinned mischievously. I stifled a laugh. She had a point. The thought of Amelia pretending to care about me was hilarious. A quick glance at Miss Lily and the smile fell from my face. The critique might have been for Amelia that time, but it could've quite easily been for me. I had to do better.

This time, I let the music get inside me. It pulsed through my veins, transforming me into Cinderella. I no longer noticed the stiffness of my new shoes against my arches. Instead, I looked at Amelia in awe, pretending I was mesmerised by the magic unfolding around me. Amelia smiled back. Caught up in the moment it was hard to tell if it was real or fake.

Amelia waved her wand theatrically above her head. In an instant, the birds appeared, circling around us in a series of elaborate jumps and turns. Khalila winked as she fluttered past. The dance of the birds was like nothing I'd ever seen. I fought against the temptation to stop dancing so that I could watch them properly. The three dancers flew across the studio floor. My adrenalin raced to keep up with them. The mirrored walls of the Academy had completely vanished. Instead, I was inside Cinderella's garden, swept up in the enchantment of the dance. For a moment, I could have sworn Khalila had wings.

Amelia grabbed my hand and together we danced side by side, perfectly in sync. I felt like she was guiding me through the dance, making sure everything went smoothly. Just like a Fairy Godmother would. It was exactly the comfort I needed.

By the time we reached the end of the scene, no one had a single breath left inside them. I hunched forward with my hands on my thighs, taking deep breaths to try and slow my heart rate down. Beside me, Khalila had flopped backwards onto the floor like a starfish, while Liam gripped onto the barre, gasping for air.

'Now that's what I want to see!' Miss Lily said, clapping her hands together. 'Though, perhaps we need to work on our stamina a bit,' she added, shaking her head at the dancers.

I grinned over at Amelia. She smiled for a moment, before looking away. Just like that, the spell was broken.

'I want you all to remember how that felt and commit like that whenever the music is playing,' Miss Lily said. She clasped her hands in front of her mouth and for a moment, seemed to disappear into her thoughts. After a minute, her head snapped in the direction of Khalila, Liam and Mya. 'Now from here, birds, you're going to cause a distraction while Cinderella is discreetly ushered offstage by our Junior ballet birds – lord help me I still need to add them into the scene. While Valentina's offstage, she'll quickly change into her tutu for the ball. It's going to be the quickest change you've ever done, Valentina. I cannot have you *late* back onto the stage.'

I cursed Anna-Maria as Miss Lily emphasised the word *late*. Obviously, she no longer trusted my time management.

Backstage, I would have less than a minute to be transformed. During that time, the Fairy Godmother and the birds would keep the audience entertained. At the end of the dance, I'd race back onto the stage in a beautiful tutu and crown, ready to be escorted to the ball. It all sounded very romantic, so long as I could pull it off.

13
Amelia

I'd be lying if I said I hadn't got a bit excited when Valentina was late to class yesterday. I'd only had time to demonstrate a few steps for Miss Lily, but dancing as Cinderella, everything felt right.

I couldn't believe Vale had been late. There was no way I'd ever be late to a standard class, let alone a production rehearsal. It was like she didn't even appreciate the fact that she'd been given the lead role.

I'll admit though, when Valentina did arrive, the rehearsal was amazing. There must have been some sort of crazy magic in the air because I actually enjoyed dancing alongside her as the Fairy Godmother. Obviously not as much as I would have if the roles had been reversed. Part of me hoped Valentina would be late again today so that Miss Lily might change the roles permanently.

I had some time to kill before the evening rehearsal, so after rushing through my homework, I decided to sneak in a bit of extra practice in my garage studio. As I marked through the steps, I let my mind wander. The Fairy Godmother's choreography was better than I'd expected. Traditionally the role was graceful and majestic, but Miss Lily's choreography was completely different. She had made the Fairy Godmother energetic and at times even sassy. She had definitely choreographed the different dances to showcase me at my best, and I was beginning to enjoy myself.

It's hard to explain, but I kind of felt guilty whenever I found myself having fun as the Fairy Godmother. It was like I shouldn't be enjoying myself because it wasn't the lead. What made it even worse was I knew I could do a better job than Valentina. Yesterday's rehearsal might have been good, but that didn't make up for all the time we'd wasted so far because Valentina couldn't remember the choreography.

It made me wonder what happened in professional companies if the lead wasn't doing a good job. Surely they would lose their role and the directors would give it to someone else. Everyone always says ballet's a cut-throat industry. You couldn't do things just to be nice, you had to make sure the performance was the best it could be. If that meant getting rid of someone who was failing to meet expectations, then so be it.

Perth Ballet Academy was a school, not a company, but it didn't change the fact that we were all striving to be professionals. Hopefully Miss Lily would treat us that way. After all, people were still paying to watch our show. I couldn't imagine they'd be very happy to watch the lead dancer make a complete mess out of things. I studied my reflection as I stepped into an *arabesque*. I forced my leg up a bit higher to try and match Valentina's flexibility. But what if Valentina didn't make a complete mess of things? She'd done a pretty good job at yesterday's rehearsal and I couldn't forget the fact that she had blown Miss Lily away with her audition.

I pushed the thought out of my mind. I needed to burn off some steam, and thankfully, there was a massive jump sequence in one of my dances that would do just that. The jumps were complicated and I wanted to practise them away from the studio, away from the judgemental eyes of people like Kate and Ava. I soared like an eagle through each of the jumps, barely letting my feet touch the floor. The higher I flew, the more I felt myself being transported away from reality and into the fairytale. My heart raced, desperately trying to keep up with the rest of my body.

Usually, the big jumps were reserved for the male solos, something to do with their centre of gravity being higher, making their jumps more impressive. The Fairy Godmother's choreography was an exception to the rule. The jumps were ginormous and my pointe shoes made them tricky. They weighed me down and made landings clunky. Miss Lily had offered for me to do some of the more dynamic routines in my soft canvas shoes, but that would have meant taking out the in-between steps that were on pointe and I didn't want that. I decided to rise to the challenge and showcase exactly what I was capable of. By the end of the performance, everyone would be talking about the Fairy Godmother, and of course, the incredible ballerina who had danced the role.

I came to a stop at the end of the sequence and dramatically waved my imaginary wand above my head. My breath burnt my chest.

Loud clapping echoed through the garage. I whirled around to see Mum standing at the door. 'Sorry, hun, I didn't want to interrupt you. You were amazing! Is that Cinderella? I've never seen jumps like that in Cinderella's choreography. She's usually much more meek and mild. Incredible! I love it!'

I smiled for a moment, enjoying the unexpected praise from Mum. Then I remembered, she wasn't praising me for dancing as the Fairy Godmother. She thought she was watching Cinderella. My shoulders dropped. I couldn't do it. I couldn't lie anymore. 'Actually, that was –' I braced myself. It was now or never. I had to tell Mum the truth about Cinderella.

'As soon as you told me you were Cinderella, I just knew you would bring something different to the role. The audience isn't going to know what hit them,' Mum said. She walked over and wrapped her arms around me.

She didn't make confessing easy, but I had to do it. Just like ripping off a Band-Aid, it would be better if I did it quickly. 'Mum, I'm not –'

'I have a surprise for you,' Mum said, once again cutting me off. She took a step back, her hands still resting on my shoulders so she could look me in the eye. 'I was going to leave it until the performance, so it didn't make you too nervous, but I just have to tell you. I spoke to my old company director, André, and when I told him you had the lead, he insisted he come and see the show. He wants to suss out your potential. It's an amazing opportunity to show him what you're capable of.'

Bile rose in my throat. I was going to be sick. This was not how things were supposed to go. The director was going to come to the show expecting to see me as the lead, only to discover it had all been a hoax. It wouldn't matter how well I danced as the Fairy Godmother. Not only was I a supporting character, but I was a liar. My career would be over before it had even begun. Who would want to hire a dancer like that? Not to mention I'd die of embarrassment. That is, if Mum didn't kill me first.

'Look at you, you're speechless,' Mum said, studying my face. 'I just knew you'd be over the moon. If you move like you just did, André will be absolutely blown away.' She kissed me on the forehead and let out a childish squeal of excitement, before making her way out of the garage.

I couldn't believe my luck. All this time I'd been chasing Mum's approval, and the one time I get it, *this* happens. I was in big trouble. There was no way out of this mess. Unless of course, I became Cinderella.

'I hope you've braced yourself for another disaster,' Ava said, as she slipped on her ballet pumps ahead of the evening's rehearsal. I had my back to Kate and Ava and, as usual, I was doing my best to ignore them. As much as I didn't need friends at ballet, I also didn't need enemies. I dragged my brush through my hair, pulling it into a tight ponytail, high on top of my head.

'Honestly, if Miss Lily insists on having Valentina as Cinderella, then she should teach her the choreography ahead of rehearsal so we don't all have to waste our time waiting for her to figure everything out,' Kate grumbled.

I twisted my ponytail into a bun and methodically began poking U-shaped hair pins in to secure it. I had a splitting headache. Not surprisingly, it had come on shortly after Mum's announcement.

'I reckon. I've got better things to do than watch Valentina stuff up the dance every two seconds. She could barely dance on pointe last week. It's actually insulting. Any one of us could do it better. I don't know why Miss Lily gave her the part,' Ava said. 'She can't even understand what Miss Lily is saying.'

'God, Amelia, it must be driving you crazy,' Kate said.

I kept my back turned. Of course it was annoying me, but there was no way I'd admit it to Kate and Ava. The pair were megamouths. Telling them would be like telling the whole world. I pretended I couldn't hear them.

'Amelia?' Kate said, sitting down on the bench beside me. 'Did you hear us? Did you see her copying you the other day? Who even does that?'

'The choreography's beautiful. I love it. Didn't you see yesterday's scene with the birds? It was amazing,' I replied, dodging Kate's question completely. I wrapped a row of small blue flowers around my bun, securing it with a tight bow underneath. It was my lucky hair tie, and at the moment, I needed every little bit of luck I could get.

'We've danced with Miss Lily since we were kids. That role should've gone to one of us,' Kate said. 'Valentina can't even do it. It's so wrong.'

'So wrong,' Ava echoed.

'It's week two of rehearsals. I wouldn't waste your time worrying about it,' I said dryly. I walked out the door before anything else could be said. Deep down, I wanted Valentina to fail, but there was no way anyone else could know that.

I was hit by a wave of disappointment as soon as I walked into the studio. Valentina was there, ready to go. She was standing barefoot next to the barre, bending one of her pointe shoes between her hands.

'New shoes?' I asked, making my way over.

'*Si*. Even after dancing with them yesterday, they are still too stiff. My toes feel like sardines,' Vale said, squeezing the toe of the shoes between her hands.

'Here,' I said, holding my hand out to take the shoe.

Vale eyed me suspiciously, but handed it over. I placed it on the ground and under her watchful eye, trod on the hard toe box with my heel. I lightly bounced up and down a couple of times, before picking up the shoe and handing it back. 'Try that,' I said.

Vale hesitated, before sliding the shoe onto her foot. 'Wow. Much better. For a moment, I thought you were going to break my shoe,' she laughed.

I couldn't help but laugh, too. I wanted to dance Cinderella, but not like that. 'I'm the Fairy Godmother. Making dreams come true,' I said with a sigh. I wandered over to the far end of the barre to warm up by myself. That was about as much *Cinderella* banter as I could muster for one day.

Today we were learning one of the most important scenes of the ballet – the Grand Ball, which of course meant the highly anticipated *pas de deux* between Cinderella and the Prince. As predicted, Sam had been cast as Valentina's Prince. The scene pretty much involved every dancer, all coupled up as ball guests. The Fairy Godmother had a small solo at the start of the ball scene, before Cinderella's coach arrived, and another once the clock had struck midnight. For the rest of the rehearsal, Miss Lily had me partnered with one of the birds, Liam, learning the *pas de deux* along with everyone else. As a partner, Liam was pretty average, but it was another opportunity to show Miss Lily what I was capable of, so I jumped at it.

'Now, boys,' Miss Lily said sternly. 'It's your job to support the girls. You need to show them off and make them look like they are princesses who weigh nothing.'

Sam scoffed and exchanged a glance with Liam. 'We're not magicians, Miss Lily.' A couple of the other boys hooted in response.

Miss Lily shot Sam a filthy look. 'No, but I am. Any more comments like that and I'll bibbidi-bobbidi-boo you out of this rehearsal.'

Nothing made me smile more than when Miss Lily put Sam back in his place. He was one of the most arrogant boys I'd ever met. Standing beside him, Valentina looked nervous. She had her hands clasped in front of her and was rocking back and forth on her heels. My guess was she'd never danced with a boy before. Lucky for me, I had. I took her nerves and used them as motivation. It was my time to shine.

When Miss Lily instructed the boys to lead us around the ballroom, I took Liam firmly by the hand and strode around the room, guiding him through the other couples.

'Amelia, pretty sure the male's supposed to lead,' Liam said. 'You're supposed to be following me.'

'Well, hurry up then,' I muttered to Liam. He was a good dancer, but he was gangly and awkward. He did okay when he was dancing by himself, but he wasn't much of a partner. Within ten minutes, I was ready to tear my hair out in frustration.

When Miss Lily announced it was time to practise lifts, I took one look at Liam's stick-like arms and shuddered. They were absolute twigs. It would be a miracle if they didn't snap when he lifted me. If he dropped me, I'd probably break a bone. Usually, I'd find the thought terrifying, but not at the moment. A broken arm would mean I couldn't do the performance and I wouldn't have to lie anymore. Problem solved.

I clenched my teeth and stepped forward into an *arabesque*. Liam awkwardly placed his hands on my hips. His grip was so weak that he may as well not have held me at all. I tightened every muscle in my body to stop myself from wobbling. Not a great start. He hadn't even lifted me yet.

'She's not a baby with a dirty nappy, Liam, hold her properly or she's going to fall,' Miss Lily yelled.

I sighed. How was I supposed to dance well if I was partnered with a complete dud? I glanced over at Valentina and Sam. They were doing okay, but their lift looked a bit awkward. I couldn't tell what was off, but it just didn't look right.

'Amelia!' Miss Lily called. I snapped to attention. 'Can you come over here for a minute and demonstrate the lift with Sam for Valentina? It doesn't look right.'

'It wasn't correct?' Valentina asked with a grimace.

'Put it this way, it looked like you were recreating the dying swan from *Swan Lake*,' Miss Lily said bluntly.

I pursed my lips to stop a smile from creeping onto my face. Personally, I didn't think the lift looked that bad, but it was better for me if Miss Lily did. Valentina looked like she wanted to curl up in embarrassment.

I marched confidently over to Sam to demonstrate. Without a word, I stepped into *arabesque*, letting Sam guide me into position. I'd danced with Sam a trillion times before and I could have done the lift with my eyes closed. I strained to lift my leg up higher, remembering I was competing with Valentina's crazy flexibility. Sam wrapped one arm around my waist and used the other to hoist my extended leg even higher into the air. In one graceful motion, I lifted my supporting foot off the ground, letting Sam sweep me forward into a fish dive. He held me there for a moment, before returning me safely back to the ground. If only Liam was as capable a partner.

Miss Lily clapped her hands. 'Now, that's what it's supposed to look like. You two, work on it, please,' she said, pointing at Valentina and Sam.

I walked smugly back to my position, locking eyes with Valentina on my way. She looked humiliated.

Cinderella, here I come.

14
Valentina

We'd been rehearsing for a few weeks now and majority of the time, I felt like I was making a complete mess of things. I wasn't used to dancing so often and I was struggling to keep up with my schoolwork. Each day, I'd rush to finish as much homework as I could in the hour between school and rehearsal, but no matter how hard I tried, I'd always end up having to stay up late afterwards to get it all done. I was exhausted.

It didn't help that I still felt awkward whenever I had to dance with Sam. We'd been working on the ball scene for over a week now and things had only slightly improved. There weren't any boys at my ballet studio back home, so it was a completely new experience for me. I wasn't scared of boy germs or anything dumb like that, I was just paranoid I was going to accidentally kick Sam or step on his toes. Plus, my armpits were kind of sweaty so he probably thought I was disgusting.

Today, I wasn't just tired, I was distracted. At the end

of class I had to ask Miss Lily if I could miss the following weekend's rehearsal. Anna-Maria's second son, Francesco, was having his first Holy Communion. According to Nonna and Papà, it would be a sin if I missed it.

'Come on, let's go again,' Sam said, after we'd stuffed up the lift for what felt like the millionth time.

I sighed and took his hand. 'Lifting me is like lifting a sack of potatoes.'

Sam laughed. 'Nah, potatoes are easier. You can throw them around and it doesn't really matter if you drop the odd one. They just bounce and roll away.'

'Do not let my Nonna hear you talk so disrespectfully about potatoes,' I said, pretending to be horrified. It was just what I needed to lighten the mood. I stepped forward into the lift and thankfully, it turned out better than the last time.

'Better, much better!' Miss Lily called across the room.

I heard Ava and Kate mutter something to one another, but I couldn't hear properly to understand the words. What I could understand, was Ava's very obvious eye roll. Over the past few weeks they'd made it pretty clear that they were annoyed about me getting the lead role. It wasn't fair. I'd auditioned just like everyone else. I shouldn't have to feel guilty for getting the part.

By the end of rehearsal, I was dripping in sweat. Thankfully so was Sam, so the grossness went both ways.

As everyone trickled out of the studio towards the change rooms, I slowly made my way over to Miss Lily. It was time to break the news that I'd be missing a rehearsal. I was doing my best to walk normally, but my whole body was aching. A quick glance in the mirror confirmed I had the swagger of a cowboy, rather than the grace of a ballerina. I did my best to straighten up.

'Excuse me, Miss Lily.' My accent sounded even stronger than usual. It happened when I was tired.

'Yes, Valentina? I'm relieved to see things are finally starting to improve with that lift,' Miss Lily said.

'Ah *si, grazie*. I have to tell you something … it is not very good.' I clasped my hands together as I spoke, twisting them around. 'My cousin, he has his first Holy Communion this Saturday. It is very important in my family. I have to miss rehearsal.'

Miss Lily's eyebrows shot up high above her glasses. She looked down her nose at me, pursing her lips. I wished I could laugh and say I was joking, but unfortunately, I was dead serious. I smiled awkwardly.

'Absolutely not,' Miss Lily said.

I studied her face, trying to figure out if she was being sarcastic. I'd learnt Australians loved sarcasm. Sometimes it didn't translate as easily for me. I'd find myself apologising to someone only to find out they were just teasing me.

Given Miss Lily was shaking her head and the frown hadn't left her face, I was fairly certain this wasn't one of those occasions.

'Valentina, we put the midyear show together in a very short amount of time. You're my lead dancer. You missing rehearsal is not an option. I'm sorry, but your family is going to have to understand that,' Miss Lily said. She grabbed her notebook and began making her way to the door, leaving me alone in stunned silence.

There was no way my family would understand or accept that a dance rehearsal was more important than a family event. A family religious event at that. I had no idea what I was going to do. It would be impossible to make it to both, and missing either one would have huge, horrible consequences. I slowly made my way towards the change room.

'Geez, who died?' Khalila asked as soon as I walked in.

'*Cosa?*' I asked. I wasn't sure if I'd missed something.

'Your face. You look like you've seen a ghost.'

'Even worse,' I said dramatically. I glanced around the change room. Amelia was over to one side, quietly fixing her hair. A couple of other girls were laughing and watching something on a phone.

'Worse than a ghost? You obviously haven't seen *The Invisible Boy*. I snuck in and watched it with my older brother and his friends. It's MA15+. Mum was furious when she found out. But *that* was terrifying.'

'I need to miss rehearsal on Saturday, but Miss Lily said I cannot,' I said glumly.

'You're right, that's much worse,' Khalila said, sitting down beside me on the change room bench. 'Girl, you can't miss rehearsal unless you're on your deathbed. Even then, if you're still breathing, it's probably not allowed.'

'My cousin Anna-Maria –' I began.

'The one who lives next door and gets offended if you don't eat her cheese?'

'*Si*, her. It is her son's first Holy Communion. In my culture, that is a very big deal. Even if it was another cousin, or a family friend, I would still be expected to go, but being Anna-Maria's family, it is … how you say … *obbligatorio*." Khalila looked confused. "I cannot … not go. They have helped us so much since we moved here. She has driven me to lots of ballet classes.'

'You know if you miss rehearsal, Miss Lily will give your role away. Probably to Amelia. You'll end up in the back somewhere,' Khalila said, glancing over at Amelia.

'Shh,' I hissed. Amelia had her back to us, but her head was tilted in our direction. She was clearly listening. Probably celebrating my misery.

'And you can't do both?' Khalila asked.

'The ceremony is at nine am. It would be impossible. Plus, there is a big family party after.'

'This Saturday's rehearsal starts at ten am. You could go to the church, then come to class, probably even rejoin the party after rehearsal.'

My heart fluttered at the possibility. 'But church will probably go for an hour and how can I get from there to here without Anna-Maria or Papà to drive me?'

'We'll pick you up. You just have to sneak out before it ends.' Khalila said it like it was the easiest thing in the world.

I sunk back against the change room wall. What other option did I have? I couldn't be in two places at once, but maybe this was the next best thing.

'Salv, I have a problem,' I said, blocking my older brother's exit on his way out the door later that night. It was after nine thirty pm.

'*Che c'è?*' he asked.

'I have to leave the church early on Saturday. So I can go to ballet rehearsal.'

'What's that got to do with me?' he asked. Salvatore and I used to be really close as kids. You wouldn't know it now.

'You sneak out all the time. I need advice on how to do it.'

'I don't sneak out. I walk out. My rules are different to yours,' he said.

'You don't say,' I said, rolling my eyes. 'How can I sneak out of church?'

'If it was me, I'd go up for Communion, take the bread, then instead of walking back to my seat, I'd walk out the door,' he said with a shrug. 'But not even I would walk out of church. If God doesn't strike you down, Nonna will. Do you really think no one will notice you disappearing?'

'You'll cover for me,' I said.

'No, I won't.'

'I would do it for you,' I pleaded.

'No, you wouldn't,' he said. He had a point. I probably wouldn't. 'Good luck.' And with that he was out the door and into the dark night.

I walked down the entry hall, stopping at the creepy Jesus/Mary picture. Mary stared back at me. 'What do I do?' I asked, staring at her face. It wasn't uncommon for my family to expect the religious statues and pictures in our house to help us out of a bind. I moved slightly and Mary grew a moustache. I made a face. Whoever thought it was a good idea to make a picture that changed like that was an idiot.

'Your thoughts look … heavy,' Mamma said, appearing in the hallway. Unlike the rest of my family, she was determined to speak English as much as possible.

'They are heavy,' I said.

'Come with me,' she said. She led me into the sitting room. Papà was at work and Giuseppe and Caterina were fast asleep, so for once, the house was quiet. The only sound that could be heard was Nonna's snoring. She'd fallen asleep in her armchair in front of the television. Mamma sat down and patted the seat beside her. I curled up against her hip, rumpling the sheet that covered the sofa. Nonna insisted we cover the sofas with old sheets so that they stayed looking new for when visitors came over. Khalila said it made our furniture look like it had been mummified.

'What is wrong?' Mamma asked, breaking the silence.

I sighed, stealing a glance at Nonna. Her mouth hung open and the light of the tv bounced off her face. She was fast asleep. I didn't know whether I should confess to Mamma that I was planning on skipping out of church. I knew she'd be disappointed, but she was also much more reasonable than Papà. It would help to have her on my side.

'It's Francesco's Holy Communion,' I said reverting to Italian. 'Miss Lily told me if I miss ballet rehearsal on Saturday, I can't play Cinderella anymore.' Miss Lily hadn't exactly said that, but I was pretty sure it was what she meant.

'That's terrible. She can't do that! That's your part,' Mamma said.

'But she can. It's not long until the performance. She needs me at every rehearsal. I'm onstage the whole show,' I said. I picked up a sheet of paper from the side table. It was covered with Nonna's signature. Line after line, her tiny name scrawled in blue pen. Despite my stress, I smiled. Nonna never went to school so she didn't know how to read or write. She had been practising her signature so she could sign documents.

'I don't know what to say. Vale, you know how much Anna-Maria and her family have done for us since we moved here. It would be disrespectful to miss Francesco's Communion,' Mamma's tired eyes looked sad. This would be hurting her as much as it was hurting me. She understood how much ballet meant to me.

'Say I went to the church, and then snuck out just before the end to get to rehearsal by ten am,' I said.

'Vale!'

'I know, it's not good. But at least I would be there for a bit. Say I did that, then came back straight after rehearsal to join the party. People might not even notice I'd left. Anna-Maria's invited the whole world, there will be so many people there,' I said.

Mamma looked thoughtfully into my eyes. I could tell she hated the idea. She was probably going to say no. To be honest, I think she was a bit scared of Anna-Maria.

Anna-Maria would kill you with kindness if you were on her good side – but she also had a bit of a savage side. She wasn't to be messed with.

'How will you get to ballet?' Mamma finally said.

I smiled. 'Khalila's family can pick me up. They will drop me back home after as well.'

Mamma sighed. '*Mamma mia*, what are we doing? Okay. I will let you. But you have to get back to the party as quickly as you can. Not a word of this to anyone. You hear me?' She rubbed her temples. 'Your Papà is going to kill me. Or worse, Nonna will.'

I hugged Mamma tightly. '*Grazie, Mamma.* I promise I won't let you down.'

15
Amelia

'Okay, Amelia, now the Fairy Godmother is ethereal, she *oozes* elegance. When you dance, it needs to be breathtaking,' Miss Lily said. She gently circled her hand in the air as she spoke, before bringing it to rest across her heart.

I was having my weekly private lesson with Miss Lily. We usually focused on technique or something I felt needed extra work, but with the midyear show just around the corner, today was a good chance to perfect things for *Cinderella*. There was nothing more challenging than a private lesson. I couldn't afford for any part of me to be out of place, or for a muscle not to be switched on. With no other students to watch, Miss Lily's eyes were firmly on me. I was expected to work hard.

The past couple of weeks had been exhausting – both physically and mentally. It was tough trying to be perfect at my role, learn Valentina's and keep the world's worst lie a secret.

I was still optimistic that Valentina wouldn't last as the lead. She was a good dancer, but she didn't seem to have the right attitude and dedication. The other day in the change room I had overheard her telling Khalila she was going to miss Saturday's rehearsal. I wouldn't even dream of missing a rehearsal. It was completely unacceptable.

I glided across the floor, lightly running on the tips of my pointe shoes. I opened my arms above my head, letting the movement flow all the way to my fingertips.

'Beautiful, Amelia. Keep those feet really close together. I don't want to see any light between your ankles. It should look like you are floating across the stage,' Miss Lily called across the room.

I smiled. I loved having Miss Lily's undivided attention. I concentrated hard to make sure I did the steps just right. I was desperate to impress her.

There was no denying that the Fairy Godmother's choreography was much harder than Cinderella's. To finish the dance, I pushed off the ground into a *grand jeté*. If someone had snapped a photo at that precise moment, it would have looked like I was doing the splits in the air. I stopped myself abruptly when I landed and reached my wand forward into my ending position.

'Almost perfect,' Miss Lily said, as she walked towards me.

'Almost?' I huffed. Standing still, I could feel the blood pumping through my thighs.

'Yes, almost. It would just be nice if I didn't hear a giant thud when you landed your *jeté*,' Miss Lily said.

I felt my cheeks burn, but smiled.

'And how do you stop the landing from being so noisy?' Miss Lily asked.

'By landing through *demi-pointe* and bending my knees,' I recited. I knew the words by heart. It was one of Miss Lily's favourite lectures.

Miss Lily laughed and placed her hands on my shoulders. 'Yes, I'm going to keep sounding like a broken record until the words are so burnt into your brain, that you actually do it,' she said. She playfully shook my shoulders.

I laughed, although I was kicking myself for my landing. I should've known better.

'Now tell me, do you like the Fairy Godmother's dances?' Miss Lily asked.

'Yeah, they're harder than I expected,' I replied honestly.

'Good, I've made them that way deliberately to challenge you. Cinderella's choreography is easier because she's onstage for longer. If it were too hard, it would be like trying to sprint a marathon. The Fairy Godmother on the other hand, comes and goes, so I can afford to make the steps more intricate. Plus, I think you can cope,' Miss Lily said.

I smiled. Of course I could cope. I was yet to find a ballet step I couldn't do. Well, except a triple *pirouette*. I had only managed to land that a few times. It killed me that I couldn't be consistent.

'That's enough for today. Keep up the good work. I want you to be so exquisite that the audience can't take their eyes off you,' Miss Lily said, beginning to walk towards the door.

'Wait, Miss Lily. Can I show you one of Cinderella's dances? I can do any one you like?' I said. I just needed Miss Lily to watch me dance Cinderella, without being distracted by Valentina, so that she would realise I was better for the part.

Miss Lily paused. 'I don't think that's necessary. You should concentrate on your own dances.'

'Oh, I am concentrating on my own. But you know, you're always saying we should push ourselves.'

'It's great you're making an effort to learn Cinderella's choreography, but don't waste too much energy. I think you know it well enough,' Miss Lily said with a frown.

'Of course I know it. By heart. But don't you want to perfect it?' I asked, following Miss Lily towards the door.

'I don't need you to be perfect as Cinderella, I need you to be perfect as the Fairy Godmother.' Miss Lily said, leaving the room.

I stopped at the door and let out a loud sigh. I felt like a complete idiot. Nagging Miss Lily was never a good idea. She probably thought I was a ballet brat now.

I didn't want to admit it, but the more I danced as the Fairy Godmother, the more I enjoyed it. If I was being completely honest, I think I even enjoyed dancing as the Fairy Godmother more than dancing as Cinderella. It was way more challenging. But it didn't change the fact that Cinderella was the lead. She hardly ever left the stage and the entire show was built around her. I had to wonder though, what would impress André more – more time onstage, or more impressive choreography?

That night, I lay flat on the lounge room floor with my legs extended up the wall. My muscles were still throbbing from my lesson and I was trying to ease the pain. I once read in a dance magazine that laying with your feet in the air helps improve circulation after a big workout, something to do with the lactic acid build-up and re-oxygenation. I wasn't entirely convinced it worked, but the position was relatively comfortable, so it was worth a shot. The pain was always worse an hour after I'd stopped dancing, when my muscles had finally relaxed. Tonight, every part of my body ached.

As I lay there, I mindlessly scrolled through social

media on my phone. I don't know why I bothered. My newsfeed's always full of the same gossip and trashy photos – girls from school pouting and holding up the peace sign, extravagant desserts – pretty much all the things I don't have time for because I'm too busy dancing. Today was no different. I stopped when I came across a post by Alice. It was a photo of her at her dance school in Singapore. She was sitting side by side with another girl in the splits, grinning at the camera. Beneath the photo was the caption #Bunheads4Life. Alice didn't share my hate for the term bunheads. It was one of the few things we disagreed on. She wore the bunhead badge with pride and was always saying I needed to loosen up a bit. I missed her.

'Tough rehearsal today, kiddo?' Dad asked, slumping down on the couch.

I glanced over at Dad.

'You know Miss Lily, she's an absolute slavedriver,' I said.

Dad chuckled. 'The better you are, the harder they push. It's when they stop giving you corrections you have to worry.'

'Huh?'

'Ah, you know, why bother correcting someone who isn't trying or isn't going to improve?'

Dad had a point. I'd never looked at it that way before.

'Plus, the lead role has to be perfect,' he said.

I grimaced. Here we go again. That stupid lie. 'Were you

the lead in most of your shows?' I asked. I'd heard a lot about Mum's dancing career, but not nearly as much about Dad's.

'Me? God, no,' Dad said. 'I got a couple of leads here and there, but there was this other guy, Christian, he was much better than I ever was. I was always either his understudy, or a supporting role.'

'*What*? But Mum said you two were always partnered together. She acts like you were a star!'

Dad laughed so hard he snorted. 'Ah, love is blind. What your mum doesn't realise, is I was only cast as her Romeo because old mate Christian twisted his ankle and couldn't dance. No need to tell her that though,' he said, tapping the side of his nose.

All this time, I had thought Dad had been the king of ballet, with Mum his queen. 'But I've even heard Mum's friends talk about your jumps. They all said you flew. You must have danced the lead enough times for people to talk about them.'

'Oh yeah, I had the best jumps in the company. I didn't need to dance the lead for people to talk about them. It didn't matter what role I was given, the choreographers always made sure it contained an epic jump sequence and I always made sure it was memorable. Easy.'

I turned my attention back to my phone. I wished it was

really that simple. I still wasn't convinced people would remember my performance if I wasn't the lead. Particularly now that it was tarnished by a lie. I was just about to put my phone down when something caught my eye. It was a video of some little ballet kids performing. One of the girls had no idea what she was doing and was stealing focus by doing her own thing entirely. Everyone was in hysterics. I chuckled for a moment, before I noticed the comments underneath the video.

@Dancer_Kate: @AvaLevitt This is where we're heading. Cinderella = Disaster-ella.

@AvaLevitt: OMG! Legit cannot stop laughing. You are so right.

@SarahMac22: HAHAHAHA!

@Jessie_Jetes: LOL you guys! She's not that bad. Some days anywayz.

@Dancer_Kate: Sadly, this would be an improvement.

@AvaLevitt: Me no speak dance.

My jaw dropped. I knew Kate and Ava were gossips, but this was nasty and it surprised me to see Sarah and Jessie getting involved. It was one thing to complain about Valentina getting the lead role because she was new, or the fact she'd been late a couple of times, but this was just catty. I actually felt sorry for Valentina.

When Saturday arrived, I had my fingers crossed that Valentina would skip rehearsal for her family thing, leaving me to dance Cinderella.

I kicked my shoes under the change room bench and began pulling my ballet clothes out of my bag. I wasn't as early as usual and behind me, a few of the other girls were getting ready for class, chatting noisily as they went.

'What are we in for today, girls?' Kate said, sauntering into the change room. She dumped her bag on one of the benches and began pulling her things out, spewing everything chaotically across the bench.

'Could go either way, but my bets are on another disaster,' Ava said.

I kept my head down, gently pulling my ballet tights up, careful to avoid putting a hole in them.

'Liam reckons she's never danced with a boy before. No wonder she looks like a complete beginner when she dances with Sam,' Sarah said.

Not Liam too. He might be an awkward *pas de deux* partner, but he was generally a nice guy. He wasn't the type to join in on the nastiness. Usually.

'Miss Lily's surely gunna change the casting soon. I mean, it was nice of her to give Valentina a chance as

Cinderella, but seriously, it's turning this production into a joke,' Ava said.

I was so busy trying to ignore the banter, that I didn't notice Khalila and Valentina enter the room.

'What are those clowns laughing at now?' Khalila asked, dropping her bag next to mine. Valentina smiled hello. So much for her missing rehearsal and me getting to dance Cinderella.

'I don't know. I do my best to block them out,' I said, glancing at Valentina. She was wearing a formal dress and looked more stressed than I'd ever seen her. Had she overheard the others teasing her on her way in?

'Talented,' Khalila said. She pulled a lime green leotard out of her bag. It was possibly the ugliest thing I'd ever seen. Khalila caught me looking and grinned, challenging me to comment.

'That's ... bright,' I said.

'I've got to stand out from the back row somehow,' she said with a wink. I had to give her some credit, I would never be as relaxed about dancing in the back as she was.

'I'm stuck,' Valentina said. Her hands were stretched behind her, fumbling with her dress zipper.

Khalila reached out to help her.

'You're very dressed up,' I commented.

'I had church. My cousin's first Holy Communion. I am

supposed to be there still,' Valentina said. Her eyes were wider than normal and she looked panicked.

'Vale's such a rebel. She skipped out on the end of church. I rescued her and brought her back to this torturous place,' Khalila said. Valentina grimaced.

'That's tough, but makes sense. You can't miss rehearsal,' I said. Although I wish she had.

Laughter erupted behind us. 'My stomach,' Mei-Lin gasped, hunched over Ava's phone. 'That's the funniest thing I've ever seen.'

'What's so funny?' Khalila asked.

Mei-Lin stifled her laugh and handed the phone back to Ava. 'Just a stupid video,' she said. Her eyes darted across to Valentina. A pink stain crept up Mei-Lin's chest and neck, before settling on her cheeks.

My arms felt tense. I knew exactly what video she was referring to. I prayed Khalila wouldn't ask anything more. If she or Valentina saw the video and read the comments, the next couple of hours of rehearsal were going to be a nightmare.

'Let me see,' Khalila asked, holding out her hand with a grin. 'I love funny videos.'

Mei-Lin shook her head at Khalila, her eyes again flickered towards Valentina.

'What? There's some hilarious stuff online. Like the

dog-shaming videos. Some of the houses have been completely trashed and the dog's just sitting there, acting all guilty.'

If only it was one of those videos. Valentina had finished getting dressed and was tying her hair up in a bun. I don't know what came over me, but I wanted to shield her from the teasing. I had to get her out of the room. Fast.

'Come on, rehearsal's about to start. We're late,' I said, ushering Valentina and Khalila towards the exit.

'Dude, chill out. I want to see the video,' Khalila said. She grabbed Ava's phone on her way past and glanced at the screen. She snorted loudly at the video. 'That's hilarious! That girl is awful!' Then she fell silent. I knew she'd seen the comments below the video. 'What's this all about?' she demanded, glaring at Ava.

'What is it?' Valentina asked, stopping at the doorway.

I placed my hand on her back and gave her a firm push, trying to get her through. Khalila looked at me. 'You knew about this?'

My jaw dropped. Her voice made it sound like it was my fault. I had nothing to do with it. I was just trying to keep the peace.

'Cool it, Khalila. As if Amelia would find a bad dancing video funny. It would probably give her nightmares,' Ava said.

Before I could stop her, Valentina reached around me and plucked the phone out of Khalila's hand. Khalila tried to grab it back, but she wasn't quick enough.

'Oh, this poor little girl,' Valentina said, watching the video. I swallowed, hoping she wouldn't scroll down to the comments. Suddenly her face changed. 'Oh. *Ho capito.*' she said quietly. She handed the phone back to Ava, studying her face. Then without a word, she turned and left the room.

Khalila glanced at me, before hurrying out after Valentina.

'Whoops!' Ava said with a grimace.

Kate scrunched up her face in mock horror. 'Well, that wasn't supposed to happen.'

I shook my head at them and left the change room. Ava was right about one thing: today was going to be an absolute disaster.

16
Valentina

I couldn't look anyone in the eye. When I woke up today, I thought my biggest problem would be sneaking out of church without Papà or the rest of the family noticing. I never expected I'd end up being the laughing stock of the whole Academy. The video was stupid and it wasn't the first time I'd ever been teased, but the past few weeks had worn me down and that was the final straw.

I wanted to prove them all wrong. I wanted to show them I was a brilliant ballerina, that I could dance Cinderella in my sleep, but the stupid video kept replaying over and over in my mind. Was I really that bad? Was my English really as awful as everyone thought? I felt like someone had reached into my stomach and twisted my insides around like spaghetti on a fork. I wished I was back home in Calabria, in the safety of my old dance studio with the run-down rooms and the creaky floorboard.

I found myself glaring at Miss Lily. Why had she put me in this position? In what crazy world had she thought it would be a good idea to cast me, the new girl, as the lead role, knowing full well I was still finding my feet and that it would turn all of the other dancers against me. To make matters worse, Miss Lily was in a horrible mood of her own that day. From the moment she barged through the studio doors, she had started barking orders at everyone.

'Valentina, pay attention. The ball is the pinnacle of the ballet, the moment of your life. I want to see joy, excitement, romance … *something*! You look like you're at a funeral, not a party,' Miss Lily yelled across the studio. 'Jessie, lift your elbows! We want lean muscles, not saggy tuckshop lady arms. Liam … Liam what have I told you about partner work? Honestly, it's like talking to a brick wall sometimes.' She threw her arms up dramatically.

Miss Lily's words all ran together. Mixed in with the loud music, they were barely distinguishable. Probably because of my bad English. I gritted my teeth and danced across the room. I tried to fake a smile, but not even that worked. I felt like knives were stabbing my toes, but for once, I wasn't ignoring the pain, I just didn't care. A few more blisters couldn't make me feel any worse than I already did. I'd disappointed my family by coming to rehearsal, and for what? No one wanted me here anyway.

Sam held out his hand and reluctantly, I took it. 'Bunhead, chill out. You're making it look like Cinderella hates the prince,' he hissed.

I felt like the walls of the studio were closing in around me. My chest ached. I wanted this so badly, so why was it going so horribly? A tear threatened to fall from the corner of my eye. I glanced at Sam. He must hate having such a terrible partner. I tilted my head back as he hoisted me into the air.

'You're lifting a delicate ballerina, Sam, not a suitcase!' Miss Lily yelled.

Sam adjusted his grip and before I knew it, I was falling. A small scream escaped my lips. With a loud grunt, Sam caught me just before I hit the floor. 'Sorry,' he murmured. 'You've gotta help me out a bit here.'

'You break it, you buy it, Sam,' Miss Lily yelled. 'It is your job to keep your partner in one piece.'

My rib hurt where Sam's fingers had caught me. I wished I could press rewind and go back to audition day. I would tell Miss Lily I appreciated the opportunity, but being my first year, I was happy with a supporting role rather than the lead. That would suck too though. I loved being Cinderella. If only I could dance Cinderella back in my hometown, where people thought I was a good dancer and didn't hate me because of it.

I breathed a sigh of relief as I pushed off into a triple *pirouette*. At least I knew that would never fail me. As

I danced past my classmates, I felt their eyes piercing through me. They were waiting for me to mess up, waiting for me to fail. I kept my eye line down and when I felt my body pulling to go faster, I let it. I raced ahead of the music, counting down until the end of the scene.

'Valentina, eyes up. People want to see your face, not the top of your head,' Miss Lily yelled above the music. 'And slow down. You're racing the music. Are you even listening?'

I was listening, but I couldn't make out her words. The roar in my ears was too loud. Coming to Australia had been a big mistake. I didn't belong here. After today, I would tell Mamma and Papà that I wanted to go home.

I threw myself into a series of fast *piqué* turns, travelling across the room. I couldn't focus my eyes enough to stop myself from getting dizzy. The room spun out of control around me, the loud music beating at my ears. I didn't see Ava coming towards me until it was too late. I smacked into her with full force, sending us both flying backwards.

'Ow!' Ava cried. 'God, watch what you're doing!'

Suddenly, there was silence. I looked up to see Miss Lily standing beside the music station, her hands on her hips. 'Would someone like to tell me what's going on here?' Miss Lily asked.

No one spoke. I looked down at my feet. I couldn't bring

myself to look back up at Miss Lily. I didn't want to see another face filled with disappointment.

'This has been by far the *worst* I have ever seen *anyone* in this class perform,' Miss Lily said. 'Aside from the fact you're all dancing like you've never attended a ballet class in your life, what I've seen today has been downright dangerous. No one is paying attention and no one is working as a team.'

Without the distraction of the music, I could understand every single word. I knew they were all directed at me.

'And Valentina, I don't know what to say,' Miss Lily said with a heavy sigh. 'That's not the Cinderella I saw at the audition all those weeks ago.'

'She must've been wearing goggles at the audition,' I heard Kate mutter under her breath to Ava. I was the only one close enough to hear them, so no one came to my rescue. Not that anyone would anyway. They were probably all thinking the exact same thing.

I stared at my pink satin pointe shoes. This was it. I prepared myself to say goodbye to dancing Cinderella. My hands were shaking and I willed myself not to cry. I couldn't let them see me cry.

'I don't know where we go from here,' Miss Lily said quietly. She removed her glasses and slowly rubbed her temples.

There was a soft knock on the door. 'Excuse me. I need … my daughter.'

My head jolted up. Papà was standing in the doorway. That was the most English I'd ever heard him speak. He'd also never stepped foot inside the Academy before. He wouldn't come unless something was wrong. I was in big trouble.

'Can I help you?' Miss Lily asked. She quickly replaced her glasses and hurried towards Papà.

'My daughter. She needs … to come to the home,' Papà said, slowly pronouncing each word and pointing at me.

I was frozen in place. I didn't know what to do. As desperate as I was to get away from such a horrible rehearsal, I knew that underneath Papà's cool exterior, he was furious. He would be putting on an act to avoid making a scene. That would be reserved for the privacy of our own home.

'We've barely started rehearsal, Mr Giorgi. We still have an hour and a half to go and from what I've seen, even that won't be enough today. It's really important all the students stay until the end, particularly my lead dancer,' Miss Lily said slowly. 'Now if you'd like to wait outside …'

I watched Papà's eyes throughout Miss Lily's speech. They were hazy and confused. I could tell he hadn't understood a word Miss Lily had said and to be honest, I don't think he cared.

'I need my daughter. Now. Thank you,' Papà said. He was polite, but firm.

Miss Lily pursed her lips. She hesitated for a moment, before nodding and motioning for me to go.

I walked silently towards the door, avoiding the judgemental eyes of my classmates.

'Hey, it's okay,' Khalila whispered as I walked past. I couldn't look at her. She was my only friend and I knew if I saw her face, I would cry.

This had been the worst day of my entire life and it was about to get even worse.

'Hurry up. Make yourself look respectable. I'll meet you in the car,' Papà said in harsh dialect as soon as we were alone in the corridor.

As I walked towards the change room, I heard Miss Lily's voice bellowing from the studio. 'Right, looks like we need a new Cinderella.'

A single tear trickled down my cheek. Game over.

17
Amelia

The entire class was in shock. I stared at the empty doorway where just moments before Valentina had exited.

'Well, that was rough,' Sam said in a low voice. I nodded. Rough was an understatement. No one had ever been pulled out of class before. I glanced around the room. Kate and Ava were whispering in the corner. One of them giggled. Honestly, the two of them made me sick.

'You saw the video?' Sam asked.

'The video wasn't the problem.'

'The comments. You know what I mean,' Sam said.

I nodded. I was listening to Sam, but in my head, I was mentally going through Valentina's choreography.

'That was low. Even for those two,' Sam said, nodding towards Kate and Ava. 'Did Vale see it?'

'Right before class,' I said. My stomach was starting to gurgle in anticipation.

Sam let out a low whistle and scratched the back of his neck. 'Uff. No wonder she tanked.'

The dancers fell silent again, everyone waiting for Miss Lily's next move. Her eyes had glazed over, deep in thought. 'What to do, what to do …' she muttered to herself.

'I'll do it,' I said, breaking the silence.

Miss Lily's head snapped in my direction. 'You'll do what?'

'I'll fill in,' I said. 'As Cinderella.'

Miss Lily let out a long sigh. 'Amelia, you're the Fairy Godmother. It makes no sense to have one lead character fill in for another.'

'It does when Cinderella's onstage for the entire show.' Somehow my voice was clear and confident. Inside my chest, my heart was galloping at break-neck speed. This was my one shot. 'Miss Lily, I know every single one of Cinderella's dances. It'll be much faster to teach someone else to be the Fairy Godmother.'

I bit my lip. Waiting. I didn't dare breathe.

Finally, Miss Lily spoke. 'Does anyone feel confident enough to give the Fairy Godmother a go?'

The studio was so silent you could have heard a pin drop. It was a rarity. Finally, Mei-Lin raised her hand. 'I know some of it. I'll try,' she said nervously.

Mei-Lin was currently dancing in the corps, she didn't have any solo parts at all. This was her big break.

'Thank you, let's give it a whirl. We'll take it slowly,' Miss

Lily said, making her way back over to the music station.

I pushed the day's events out of my head. This was exactly what I had been preparing for. If I wanted to win the part of Cinderella, it was now or never. As terrible as I felt for Valentina, I couldn't let myself get caught up in the drama. I had problems of my own.

'Now, we've had enough drama for one day, let's try and get through the rest of rehearsal without any more,' Miss Lily said with a glance over her shoulder. 'Hopefully, Valentina will be back by Monday, but today is proof that we need to have a backup plan.'

As the opening bars of the ballroom scene filled the room, I stepped onto pointe and did exactly what I was trained to do. I moved easily through the choreography. With all the practice I'd put in, I could do the entire performance in my sleep. My muscles snapped into gear, knowing exactly what was expected of them. I was relieved when I felt Sam's hand guiding me through the pas de deux. Unlike Liam, he knew exactly how to support a dance partner, and together we danced effortlessly.

'Very nice, you two!' Miss Lily yelled above the music. 'But I need to see it in your faces. Right now, you're Sam and Amelia. I need to see the Prince and Cinderella.'

Hearing the words made my heart flutter. I am *Cinderella*. I forced a smile onto my lips, repeating the words again.

I am *Cinderella*. I should have been over the moon, but something didn't feel right. My body went through the motions without much thought, but inside I suddenly felt flat. I had to keep reminding myself to smile.

A loud chime sounded in the music and the rest of the dancers froze. Midnight. Pretending to be the Fairy Godmother, Mei-Lin danced through the frozen ball guests towards me. Cinderella's time at the ball had run out. I danced away, fighting the spell that would destroy Cinderella's dress and turn her coach into a pumpkin. No one else moved a muscle, making it seem as if time stood still.

I cringed. Mei-Lin was making a complete mess of the Fairy Godmother's choreography. *My* choreography. I couldn't exactly blame her – it wasn't like she'd secretly been learning the role in the hope that I'd get sick – but still, she was a mess.

As the scene came to an end, I dashed off the imaginary stage, leaving behind a pointe shoe. As soon as I was gone, the rest of the dancers came back to life, just in time for the Prince to discover the forgotten shoe. The music ended and everyone stared expectantly at Miss Lily.

'Well,' she said with a pause.

I wiped the sweat up my forehead and into my hair. I was exhausted.

'That wasn't terrible, but it needs a lot of work. Amelia and Mei-Lin, well done for stepping in at such short notice. Grab a quick drink, then I want everyone to go over things. Amelia, help Mei-Lin if she needs it, please.'

I nodded as I walked towards my pigeonhole. I grabbed my sweat towel and dabbed at my face.

'Got what you wanted, hey Amelia?' Kate said, grabbing her drink bottle. She took a big swig and smiled smugly at me.

'Sorry?' I said.

'Casting is as it should be,' Kate said. 'Well, kind of. Obviously I should be Cinderella, but at least it's not a new student now.'

I didn't know what to say. I might have wanted the role of Cinderella, but what had happened to Valentina hadn't been what I'd wanted at all. The last thing I wanted was for Kate and Ava to think I was on their team. I avoided Kate's expectant eyes and began to walk away. Something was niggling at my stomach. I stopped and glanced back at Kate. 'You should get rid of that stupid video and those comments,' I said sharply. I turned on my heel and headed for Mei-Lin before Kate had a chance to reply. It went against everything I'd ever believed in about getting involved in Academy drama, but this time, something had to be said.

18
Valentina

It's a pain that's indescribable. When you realise you can't have the thing you want more than anything else in the world. It seeps through your body and fills every single part of you.

At first, Papà and I sat beside one another in the car in complete silence. I wanted to apologise, but I also wanted him to understand that I hadn't had a choice.

'You were practically fluent when you spoke English to Miss Lily,' I finally said, trying to lighten the mood. Dumb move. It was as if Papà didn't hear the compliment, or didn't want to. Instead, he used it as an opportunity to start talking.

'You disrespected me. Not just me, the whole family. Anna-Maria's family, too,' he spat the words out in Italian and they stung. His hands were firmly holding the steering wheel, but it felt as if I'd been slapped across the face.

'I didn't want to,' I said. It was true. It was the last thing I'd wanted to do.

'Today was an important day for the family and you chose dance instead. Your priorities are all wrong. They have been since we moved here. We should never have come.'

After today's rehearsal, part of me agreed with him. Maybe we shouldn't have come. Maybe we should have stayed in our old-fashioned little town, where no one ever pushed the boundaries or challenged themselves. Where my classmates thought I was a good dancer and never begrudged me for it. But then again, if we'd stayed, maybe I would have had to give up ballet soon anyway. Either way, my time had run out.

'You spend all your time at that ballet school. You never have time for the family. We don't see you,' Papà continued.

That part made me angry. I had never before spoken back to Papà, but a fire built inside me and exploded out before I had a chance to stop it. 'You never see me? That's because you're at work when I'm at home. What about Salvatore? He's never home. At least you know where I am.'

'This isn't about your brother,' Papà snapped.

'It never is. He has his own set of rules and it's not fair. We came to Australia for opportunities, well I'm doing something I love more than anything else in the world. I work so hard at ballet, I deserve the rewards that come with it. You say I don't have time for my family? Every single night I wipe Caterina's tears and stroke her head until she falls asleep. I push her and Giuseppe to speak English, so they don't get behind at school. Ballet is my only escape.'

Papà was silent for a moment, stunned by my outburst. 'You never spoke to me like that in Italy. Australia has been a bad influence on you. It's made you disrespectful. Giuseppe said you failed a history test. You're right, we came for opportunities, but we came for opportunities that help with our future. Ballet won't help. School will. And you're not taking that seriously.'

I cursed Giuseppe for telling Papà about my failed test. I don't even know how he knew about it. The test had been crumpled down the bottom of my backpack. 'I did study. I tried my best but it is hard in another language.' The test had been all about Australia's involvement in World War II. I knew all about Italy's involvement, but Australia's was new to me. Memorising the facts in another language was tough. The teacher wasn't even mad when she returned my test. She understood. I was about to tell Papà that, but he'd already moved on. When he was mad, it was impossible to keep up.

'You think no one noticed you disappear today? Anna-Maria is very offended. After all she's done for you. Driving you to and from dance. Mamma told her you weren't feeling well, but she knew you went to ballet.'

Based on Papà's reaction and the amount of times he'd used the word disrespect, you would think I'd spat on Anna-Maria. 'I'll apologise and explain to Anna-Maria. She'll understand.'

'From now on. No more ballet.'

'What?'

'Enough is enough. You've had your fun. Now it's time to be serious. You go to school, you study and you spend time with the family. That's it.'

'But the midyear show? I'm the lead.' At least, I was the lead. I wasn't so sure after today's rehearsal.

'Valentina, don't argue. I've made my decision.'

I sunk back into my car seat. I felt like someone had pulled a plug and let all of the air out of my body.

If I were Australian, none of this would have mattered. I cursed the Southern Italians for their rigid values. There was more to life than family, food and tradition. It didn't matter how important ballet was for me — if it wasn't right for the family, it wasn't right for me. Just like that, I was done.

'Vale's back!'

I'd planned on making a discreet entrance at Ciccio and Anna-Maria's. Caterina had other plans. She raced across their backyard and leapt into my arms, knocking the wind out of me. I clutched at her, fighting every urge to cry into her hair.

'Did you dance?' she asked loudly.

I shushed her. Too many eyes were staring at me. 'Not now, Cate,' I said, placing her back down on the ground.

'I'll tell you a secret,' she said, tugging on my arm to get me to bend down to her level. I obliged, ignoring the questioning looks from the rest of the family. She had one hand cupped around her mouth as she whispered her treasured secret. Sadly, it was cupped in the wrong direction so everyone could see her lips moving and hear exactly what she was saying. 'Giusé ate the Jesus bread,' she said.

'What do you mean Giuseppe ate Communion?' I asked, searching for my little brother in the crowd.

'He stole it off Pino,' she said with a grin and a nod. Pino is Anna-Maria's ten-year-old son. His name's short for Giuseppe. Given there are a lot of name double-ups in our community, we use a lot of nicknames.

'That's not good,' I said, knowing if Mamma or Nonna found out, our Giuseppe would get a clip over the ear.

'Ah … the ballerina returns,' Anna-Maria said, raising her eyebrows at me.

'I'm sorry,' I said, and I meant it. I was sorry. Sorry I couldn't be in two places at once.

'These kids. They move country, get a taste of freedom and they forget the things that are most important,' Anna-Maria said, waving her hand in the air in that stupid regal way she did.

I felt anger boiling inside me again. I glanced around the backyard. Salvatore was standing over to the side with a group of the older boys. For the first time in my entire life, I hated him. I hated how easy he had everything. How he could do whatever he liked and no one ever batted an eyelid. He would always be the favourite. King Salvatore. He never helped around the house, or looked after the younger kids and God knows how many dinners he'd missed. The times he did show up, Nonna would act like royalty had arrived, roll out the red carpet and cook him his favourite meal. It wasn't fair.

'Vale, go and get the tray of desserts. Offer them around,' Anna-Maria ordered.

I nodded and off I went, obediently like Cinderella. I was loading up a tray of pastries in the kitchen when Mamma appeared.

'Vale, I tried to keep the secret,' she whispered, wrapping an arm around me. 'You know what everyone is like. They have twenty sets of eyes. They see everything.'

'Papà won't let me dance anymore,' I said. My lip quivered as the words came out.

'Not now, Vale. Hold your head high. We'll talk about this later, behind closed doors.'

Behind closed doors. The place where arguments belong, because God forbid anyone thought our family was any less than perfect.

It was eleven o'clock before we finally walked next door to our own house. The party had gone all day and late into the night. Once again, I found myself questioning what difference missing a couple of hours during the day had actually made. To any normal family, none at all. For the first time in ages, I was completely alone in my bed. Across the room, Caterina was snoring softly in her own bed. I grabbed an extra pillow and snuggled into that instead. It was too late at night to try and talk to Papà about ballet, and I didn't think it would make any difference anyway. Papà's a typical Calabrese *con la testa dura* – with a hard head. Once he'd made a decision, it was final. I wished I hadn't gone to rehearsal today. I probably would have lost my role as Cinderella, but at least I wouldn't have lost ballet altogether.

The moon shone through the window, illuminating the framed photo on my bedside table. It was of me and my dance class back home. We were all dressed in purple tutus, hugging one another. I swallowed down the lump that had formed in my throat. I needed my friends back home, Maestra Anna and the tiny little dance studio with the creaky floorboard. I hadn't felt homesick since we'd moved to Australia, but now it was as if I had been engulfed in a wave of it.

I thought about the stupid video on Ava's phone. I knew I was a better dancer than the one I'd been over the past few weeks.

I used to think it didn't matter what language you spoke in a dance class. Dance was a universal language spoken through the body. I was wrong though. It did matter. The chaos of words crashing through my head made it impossible to lose myself in the music. They weighed me down, making it hard to move properly. As difficult as it was, I didn't want to give up ballet. I didn't know who I was or how to exist without it. Dance was such a big part of me, that without it, I worried I'd turn into a ghost. I hugged my pillow tighter. I'd never felt more alone. A strangled sob escaped me and finally, the tears gushed out.

19
Amelia

Two full weeks had passed since Valentina had been pulled out of class. No one had heard a word from her, not even Khalila. As a result, my wish had come true. I was filling in as Cinderella and as time went by, it seemed it might stay that way.

At home, I felt like a weight had been lifted off my shoulders. No more lying. I could actually talk about ballet without wanting to throw up.

At the Academy though, things were just plain weird.

'Miss Lily should've known from the start that it was safer to stick with the students she *actually* knew and trusted,' Ava said, as she and Kate passed me during rehearsal. I'd never seen eye to eye with the pair, so I had no idea why they were suddenly so supportive of me dancing as the lead.

'Okay, Amelia and Mei-Lin, run the dance from the top,' Miss Lily said, restarting the music. 'I want to see more emotion this time. A blank face is a boring face.'

Mei-Lin was still doing an awful job of dancing as the Fairy Godmother. She'd done a pretty good job of picking up the choreography so quickly, but the steps were way too hard for her and her transitions were clunky. I cringed every time I saw her. There was nothing graceful about her performance whatsoever. She looked like a baby giraffe learning how to walk.

I danced Cinderella with ease. There were a lot of little steps, but they weren't overly complicated. Miss Lily had been right, Cinderella was a marathon, the Fairy Godmother was a sprint. I knew the choreography by heart, but my main challenge was making sure I had enough stamina to get through it all. I performed the steps, doing my best to avoid looking at Mei-Lin. If I couldn't see her, I could pretend she wasn't butchering my beautiful dances.

When the music came to an end, I held my position for a moment, before relaxing to catch my breath. I stole a quick glance at Mei-Lin. Part of her hair had come loose from her bun. She looked scruffy and completely overwhelmed.

'Amelia, that was good. Mei-Lin, I know you're still new to this role and the choreography is a lot, but you need to work harder please,' Miss Lily said firmly. 'I don't want to have to simplify anything.'

I cringed. It would kill me if the choreography had to be

simplified. It was too good for that to happen.

'Everyone take five. Go over anything you're unsure of. Mei-Lin, I'm looking at you,' Miss Lily said, her finger pointed towards Mei-Lin as she left the room.

Khalila sidled up beside me. 'You know this is ridiculous, right?' she said.

I furrowed my brow and looked her up and down. Today, she was wearing a purple-and-blue tie-dye leotard, with her hair in two little buns, high on top of her head. 'You mean what you're wearing?'

Khalila grinned. 'You'd think that would offend me, but it doesn't. This class needs a bit of colour. No, this casting's ridiculous. Mei-Lin isn't any more suited to the role of Fairy Godmother than you are to Cinderella. It's all wrong.'

'What do you mean? I'm dancing just fine as Cinderella,' I snapped.

'Exactly, *fine*. Not great. As the Fairy Godmother, you're amazing. The Fairy Godmother was choreographed for you. Cinderella wasn't,' Khalila said.

I glared at her. No one had ever described my dancing as *fine* before. Fine was how you described an average dish at a disappointing restaurant. I was doing great as Cinderella. Khalila couldn't do half the things I could, so who was she to judge?

'What happened at Vale's last rehearsal was horrible. She tanked because the whole Academy was against her,' Khalila said.

'Well, she needs to get thicker skin. This is ballet, not lawn bowls. If she can't handle criticism, she's in the wrong place,' I said. I crossed my arms and avoided Khalila's eyes. I knew the gossip and teasing had been more than just criticism, but I wasn't going to start having a heart-to-heart with Khalila about it.

'Whatever, Amelia. What happened to Vale wasn't just criticism. You tell yourself whatever you need to hear to be okay with the fact that you took Vale's role, but you and I both know that if she'd been given a proper chance, she would've made a fabulous Cinderella.'

My jaw dropped. Who did Khalila think she was? She was completely out of line. 'I didn't *take* the role. Miss Lily asked me to step in. I'm just trying to help,' I said defensively. Tension rippled along my arms and into my clenched fists.

'Maybe so, but you can't tell me you've exactly been nice to Vale since she was cast as Cinderella. Everyone's been jealous from the beginning just because she's new here and crazy talented. You always bang on about how you're a professional and you want to be treated like one. Well, do you think a *professional* company wouldn't give a dancer the lead role just because they were new? And do you think the other dancers would dare complain if they did?'

I pursed my lips, but didn't say anything. It was a point I couldn't argue with.

'I didn't think so,' Khalila said. She walked back to join the other birds.

I knew she was right, but it didn't change anything. Valentina hadn't shown up for class. That wasn't my fault. I was just doing what I was asked to do. Was I happy to dance Cinderella? Yeah, of course. But it still wasn't my fault.

I saw Sam across the studio and made a beeline for him. I needed to practise instead of wasting my time worrying about things that were out of my control.

'We need to go over the *pas de deux*. It's a mess.'

Sam winced. 'That's no way to ask a gentleman to dance, Amelia.'

'Funny, I don't see any gentlemen around here,' I said, narrowing my eyes at him.

Sam dramatically returned my glare. 'Ask nicely,' he said with a smirk. He crossed his arms and tapped his foot on the ground.

'You're kidding, right? Just pick up from the turn sequence in Act Two's ball scene,' I said.

'Has anyone ever told you that you take the fun out of ballet?' Sam said, but he did what he was told.

We began a series of turns across the room. 'It would be great if you did the turns properly,' I hissed mid-turn. I knew I was being unfair. I was taking my anger out on Sam and he wasn't really doing anything wrong. As much as I hated to admit it, Khalila had struck a nerve.

Sam suddenly grabbed my hand and pulled me back towards him. I braced myself as he hoisted me high above his head into an elegant lift, before dropping me down into a fish dive. I let out a small gasp as my torso flew towards the ground. I came to a sudden stop, my face hovering inches above the floor. I was impressed. Sam made lifts effortless.

Sam straightened back up and gently lowered my front leg onto the tip of my pointe shoe. I extended my back leg out into an *arabesque*, creating a picture-perfect angle.

'I don't think you need to worry about me doing my role correctly, *bunhead*,' Sam said.

'The lift doesn't go that high,' I said through gritted teeth. I'd never admit to Sam that he was an amazing dancer. His ego would go into overdrive.

'It's more impressive though, don't you think?'

Before I could argue, Sam and I were pushed roughly from the side. I slipped off the tip of my pointe shoe and stumbled. Sam quickly caught me.

'I'm so sorry!' Mei-Lin shrieked. 'I was concentrating so hard on my turns I didn't see you.'

I curled my upper lip. 'I think you should concentrate a bit harder. The turns don't even travel in this direction,' I snapped.

'*Rowwww!*' Sam said, pretending to hiss like a cat. 'Settle down, ladies.'

I scowled. Mei-Lin was completely ruining my Fairy Godmother solos. At the rate she was going, the choreography would end up being changed to something basic. It was heartbreaking. The audience needed to be wowed by the entire performance. At the moment, the show was a dog's dinner.

A chuckle from Sam interrupted my thoughts. I followed his eye line to where Mei-Lin was now practising one of the dynamic jump sequences. She stumbled between steps, tripping over her own feet, before clumsily doing a *jeté*, which barely made it off the floor.

I threw back my head and groaned. Why did I have to fix everything? I stormed towards Mei-Lin. 'Mei-Lin, that's not the choreography. God, have you practised at all?'

Mei-Lin huffed loudly. 'There are too many stupid little steps. It's impossible. It would look much better if –'

I cut her off. '*If* you actually practised and did the correct choreography.'

'You know what, at the moment it's my role, not yours. So back off,' she said, angrily.

We fell silent as Miss Lily re-entered the room. 'Places!' she yelled.

Mei-Lin and I glared at one another, before returning to our starting positions. Everything was falling apart and I couldn't stop it.

I covered my ears and took a deep breath. Khalila and I had stayed back after class to help Miss Lily with the Junior ballet rehearsal. When I'd agreed to help, I didn't realise it meant sacrificing my sanity. I was surrounded by a bunch of younger kids who were driving me absolutely nuts. Miss Lily had left us in charge of warm-up. I was beginning to question whether I'd survive long enough to see the actual rehearsal.

Khalila was worse than all of the little kids put together. She was circling the studio with a train of kids in tow. They were all flapping their arms and squawking like birds.

'That's great! You're really getting into character. Be the bird!' Khalila yelled above the racket.

I grabbed her arm as she scuttled past.

'Hey Milly! How good do my baby birds look?' Khalila asked enthusiastically.

'First of all, don't call me that. Second of all, this is a ballet rehearsal, not the zoo. Keep them quiet until Miss

Lily gets back, or I'm gunna lose my mind,' I said through gritted teeth.

Khalila just laughed and continued to circle the room. 'We're getting into character. You should try it,' she called over her shoulder.

I'd only been in the room for ten minutes and I was already stressed to the max. The Academy was meant to be my happy place. My sanctuary. Khalila and her bunch of birds were completely ruining it. If I didn't call the room to order soon, things would turn ugly.

I took a step forward and clapped my hands loudly like Miss Lily always did. 'Okay birds, that's enough. Fly back down to earth right now!'

The birds stopped squawking and dropped their arms. They looked nervously at one another.

'Do as she says, and none of us will get hurt,' Khalila said, holding up her arms to surrender. The younger dancers giggled.

I placed my hands on my hips and raised my chin. I needed these kids to understand I was the boss. The insanity had to stop. 'In a couple of weeks time, we'll be in the theatre for rehearsals. If you don't take this seriously, you'll be offstage,' I said firmly.

These kids had to learn that ballet was a serious, disciplined art. They weren't running around on a footy oval. If they wanted to be professionals one day, they had to start acting like one now.

Khalila sidled up next to me. 'Probably a bit harsh there, Milly. These kids are only like, eight.'

I quietened her with a look. 'Okay, Juniors. Are your legs warm? Show me the splits with your right leg forward,' I instructed.

I decided to do ballet bootcamp until Miss Lily returned. It was something Mum always did with the younger kids at the school she taught at. The kids obediently slid down into the splits. The room was dead quiet. *Exactly* how a ballet studio should be.

I walked along the line like a drill sergeant, issuing orders to each child. 'Point your toes. Square up your hips. You've got the wrong leg.' It was the most fun I'd had all day. Perhaps if ballet failed, I could join the army.

I stopped in front of a little girl with strawberry blonde hair. The girl was hovering about ten centimetres above the ground, balancing her weight on her hands. Her face was contorted in pain.

'Is that as far as you can go?' I asked, crouching down beside her.

The little girl nodded glumly. 'But my left leg is flat,' she said defensively.

'What's your name?'

'Georgie.'

'We have two legs, Georgie, you can't just focus on one. You need to work really hard to get both flat, okay?'

Georgie nodded again.

I stood back up and began counting down from ten to one.

'I think the power's gone to your head a bit, Sergeant,' Khalila said.

As soon as I reached the number one, the kids collapsed out of the splits. A chorus of relieved sighs filled the air.

'Left leg!' I immediately yelled.

The kids groaned, but obeyed orders. This time, Georgie stretched out easily into her splits. She beamed proudly up at me, so I gave her the thumbs up. I might have sounded mean before, but I still remembered how happy I'd been when I finally had my splits flat.

Once they had done the splits twice in each direction, I told them to stretch quietly until Miss Lily arrived. I extended my right leg out to the side, lifting it as high into the air as it would go without using my hands. I held my arm firmly in second position for balance, straining to lift my leg higher and higher. I could feel someone watching and glanced over my shoulder to see Georgie standing behind me.

'You're not Cinderella in the dance, are you?' she asked.

I pursed my lips. 'At the moment, yes, I am.'

'Oh, I thought the new girl was? Valentina? I know *all* the big girls' names,' she said proudly.

I smiled. I was the exact same when I was a kid. The older students had been my idols. 'She was. It's a bit complicated. She's gone on a bit of a holiday. I guess if she comes back, she'll be Cinderella and I'll go back to being the Fairy Godmother.'

Georgie twisted her lips in thought. 'She went on a holiday? You can't do that during rehearsals. I bet she's in big trouble,' she said, raising her eyebrows dramatically. And with that, she skipped back over to join her friends.

Georgie was right. Vale was in big trouble and the way things were going, so was the Academy and the entire production.

20
Valentina

I hadn't danced in two weeks. My muscles felt stiff and my heart felt heavy. When I wasn't at school, I spent my time wandering around the house in a daze. I felt completely lost. Caterina loved having me home more, but even she was upset that I wouldn't get to be Cinderella anymore. Her dream had been crushed along with mine.

It was Saturday night and I'd stayed up late watching *Don Matteo* on SBS with Nonna. She was obsessed with the show and shushed me whenever I tried to speak during it. I think she had a crush on Don – the crime-fighting priest.

I was just about to go to bed when I heard the front door quietly open and close. I peered out into the hallway and gasped.

'*Che cavolo* … what the heck happened to your face?' I said to Salvatore.

One of his eyes was swollen and his lip was bleeding. 'Nothing,' he grunted, pushing past me towards the bathroom.

I grabbed a bag of frozen peas, before following after him. I tapped on the door, before gently opening it. Salvatore was hunched over the sink. It was hard to tell with his swollen eye, but it looked like he'd been crying.

'Here,' I said, holding out the peas.

He glanced over at me, before reluctantly taking them. I turned to go, but then stopped. 'What happened?' I asked.

He looked at me in the reflection of the mirror. 'You wouldn't understand.'

I made my way into the bathroom and perched on the side of the tub. 'Try me.'

Salvatore held the peas over his eye with one hand, while pressing tissues against his bleeding lip with the other.

'Here,' I said. I stood up and grabbed a bottle of antiseptic out of the bathroom cabinet. With a cotton bud, I gently dabbed at the cut on Salvatore's lip. I didn't think he was going to answer my original question, but finally, he spoke.

'It's easy here for you. You don't know what it's been like for me,' he said, flinching away from the sting of the antiseptic.

'Easy?' I scoffed. 'You think it's easy for me? Papà has me under house arrest. I can't even dance. You get to do whatever you like.'

'So, you can't dance? Big deal. At least you speak English. You fit in here. I'm like a fish without water. I open my mouth and people laugh,' Salvatore looked away, as if avoiding my eyes. 'Or hit me.'

'Someone hit you because your English is bad? *Uffa* ...'

'Because my English is so bad, it's offensive. And because I'm different to the Australian boys. They get annoyed because their girlfriends like my accent, and then they mistake my friendliness for flirtation. As if I would steal someone's girlfriend.'

I grimaced. '*Uffa*,' I repeated. I didn't know what else to say. I could try and help Salvatore with his English, but that was only if he wanted to learn. I studied his face again. 'Mamma will go crazy when she sees your face. *Oh dio*, Nonna will have a heart attack. You might actually kill her.' I feigned horror.

'Don't say that. It's not funny to speak about dying,' Salvatore said.

I rolled my eyes. My family was very superstitious. Any mention of the word death made them panic. It was as if the word alone was enough to put the *malocchio* – the evil eye – on them.

'With a face like that, the Australian boys have nothing to worry about,' I said with a cheeky grin, heading for the door. 'No way will their girlfriends think you're good-looking. You're uglier than a pirate.'

Salvatore glared at me with his one good eye. '*Grazie*, that's very kind.'

I paused at the doorway. 'If you were home more, I'd help you with your English. It's not like I have anything else to do,' I said, suddenly feeling flat again.

'Vale,' Salvatore said, turning to face me properly. 'It won't last forever, Papà being angry. You'll get to dance again. You'll see.'

I sighed. If only he were right.

As predicted, Mamma and Nonna had a fit when they saw Salvatore's face the following morning. Nonna acted like it was the Pope who had fallen ill, while Mamma flew into a crazy fit of rage. She whipped Salvatore across the arm with a tea towel, yelling about how stupid he was for going out all the time in a country he didn't understand. Caterina, Giuseppe and I watched on in amusement. I had a feeling Salvatore wouldn't be going out as much anymore.

Mamma and Nonna's main concern was what the neighbours would think when they saw Salvatore. It was a huge day for our street. It was *Pig Day*. All of our Italian neighbours had congregated in our backyard to make sausages. I was pretty sure my Australian friends just bought theirs from the supermarket, but not our community. Instead, each year we bought a couple of dead pigs and spent the day turning them into sausages. It's a pretty gross process if you're not used to it.

Our house was bursting at the seams. I'd never seen so many people in the one place. All of the men were busy making the sausages, while the women prepared lunch for everyone. As usual, the kids just ran amuck.

'*Bella mia*, go and get the salt,' Papà called to me. I fetched the salt and when Papà told me to throw a handful of it into the minced meat, I obliged. When I was younger, I'd asked if there was a recipe for the sausages. Everyone acted like it was the funniest question in the world. There was no such thing as a precise measurement, like a tablespoon or a cup. They worked on handfuls, and how the mixture looked to the eye – *quanto basta*.

Papà worked his hands through the mixture, massaging the meat. '*Grazie, principessa*,' he said. He leant back to plant a kiss on my forehead. I think he was starting to feel guilty about the whole ballet situation. He'd been excessively sweet to me all week as if to make up for it. He obviously didn't feel guilty enough to remove the ballet ban, just guilty enough to suck up.

'Good to see your hands dirty for once,' I said to Salvatore. He was at the other side of the tub of meat, copying Papà. He made a face, which only made me laugh even more. His left eye had swollen completely shut overnight. He looked horrible.

'*Chi vuole un caffè?*' Mamma yelled. She was carrying a metal tray full of coffee cups with a giant moka pot nestled in the middle.

The men whose hands were full of meat groaned about bad timing. The others eagerly flocked around. 'Vale, hand these out, will you?' Mamma said, handing me cups of coffee.

Papà called me over. 'Pour a bit of coffee into my mouth, *bella mia.*' His hands were still deep in the sausage mince. I gently blew on his cup of coffee to cool it down, then standing on my tippy-toes, I held the cup up to his lips.

'Ah!' He said, puckering his lips together as he finished. 'This is why you're my favourite,' he said with a wink.

Despite myself, I smiled. I couldn't stay angry at Papà. He was hurting me more than he realised, but he was still Papà.

'Vale, that girl is back here. With another one!' Giuseppe yelled, racing across the patio towards me.

'What girl?' I asked. I followed the direction of his finger. My breath caught in my throat as I spotted Khalila and Amelia, standing awkwardly next to Nonna. Nonna was pushing a tray of biscuits at them. I weaved my way through the crowd to rescue them.

'*Che ci fate qua?*' I asked. They both stared at me blankly. I shook my head. I'd been speaking Italian all day and sometimes it was hard to switch between languages. 'What are you doing here?'

'Your Nonna invited us in,' Khalila announced proudly.

'My Nonna? The one who doesn't speak a word of English?'

'Sure she does! She said *Hel-lo, how are yoooou*?' Khalila said, putting on a thick Italian accent. I couldn't help but laugh. So even Nonna had been secretly learning English!

'But why are you here?' I asked again. Khalila looked bizarrely at home amongst the crowd of Italians. Amelia on the other hand, looked completely out of place. She looked around, her eyes as wide as pizzas.

'We came to get you back,' Khalila said.

I tilted my head towards Amelia, who wasn't paying attention, and raised my eyebrows.

'Surprisingly, it was her idea,' Khalila said, returning my shocked expression.

'It was *your* idea to get me back to the Academy?' I asked, clicking my fingers in front of Amelia to get her attention.

She sighed. 'Yes. The show's a complete disaster. No one knows what they're doing with all of the role changes. Things need to go back to how they were.'

If someone had told me this morning that Amelia would come to my house, asking me to return to dance

Cinderella, I would have said they were dreaming. I was completely shocked.

'*Ciao*, Khalila,' Out of nowhere, Mamma appeared. She planted a kiss on each of Khalila's cheeks, before turning to Amelia. 'Sorry, *bella*, we have not met.'

'I'm Amelia. What's everyone doing here?' Amelia asked. It was as if she was completely hypnotised by sausage-making day.

'It's pig day. We're making sausages,' I explained.

'You are both just in time for lunch,' Mamma said. 'Come help me dish up. The extra hands will be very good.'

Salvatore and the other young boys had spread long fold-out tables across the backyard. I had no idea where they'd all come from, but there was enough room to accommodate the entire street. Anna-Maria began flinging cloths across the tables and within minutes, they were set, ready to feed our sausage-making army.

'Girl, this is insane!' Khalila said. I laughed. I guess it was a bit.

Mum filled our hands with bowls piled high with spaghetti, which we quickly spread around the table. Before long, work had stopped and everyone was seated together.

'What's that?' Amelia whispered, pointing at a bowl in the middle of the table.

I smiled, knowing my response would most likely gross

Amelia out. 'That is a bowl filled with the parts of the pig that cannot be used for sausages. Like the bones if they still have a tiny bit of meat on them, the skin … and the feet.'

As predicted, Amelia scrunched up her face. 'Feet? Ick.'

'Dare you to eat one,' Khalila said with a grin.

Amelia rolled her eyes and ignored her. 'They've made a lot of sausages. What are they all for, like a really big barbecue or something?'

Mamma overheard her. 'Some we will cook. Others we will hang in the shed to dry out. Those are my favourite,' she said with a warm smile.

Papà took his seat at the head of the table. He noticed Khalila and Amelia for the first time. 'Hel-lo,' he said slowly, his cheeks turning bright red with the effort of speaking English.

'This is Khalila and Amelia. From the ballet academy,' I explained in dialect. Papà nodded slowly, then smiled politely at the girls.

'You are hungry?' Papà asked. 'Vale, get them more food.'

'Their bowls are still full,' I protested. One of the ladies from down the street jumped to her feet and started spooning potatoes and roasted capsicum onto a side dish for the girls. Amelia was completely lost for words, Khalila accepted the plate happily.

'Why are they here?' Papà asked me in dialect.

I hesitated. 'They want me to return to ballet.'

Papà took a mouthful of his spaghetti, slowly chewing it.

'Khalila!' Caterina yelled from the other end of the table. Khalila waved in her direction. 'These are Vale's ballet friends,' she explained to the rest of the table.

'You ballerinas need to eat more. Do you like the pasta? Here, do you want some bread?' Anna-Maria said, passing bread across the table. Amelia tried to wave it away, but a piece of bread landed on the side of her plate regardless.

'Leave the girls alone, Anna,' Mamma said.

'What do you do in *Cinderella*?' Caterina yelled down the table. The yelling wasn't overly necessary. An Italian feast had never been quieter. Everyone was either busy eating or trying to eavesdrop on our conversation.

'I'm a magical bird,' Khalila explained. 'And Amelia here is usually the Fairy Godmother, but unless your sister comes back, she'll dance as Cinderella.'

Caterina scrunched up her face, trying to understand Khalila's fast English. I quickly translated. Caterina's face lit up. 'Oh, Vale is the best Cinderella. Sorry,' she said, looking at Amelia.

Despite the cool winter air, my cheeks were warm. I didn't know how this conversation was going to play out. I watched Papà's face, doubting he was understanding the English.

'You're right,' Amelia suddenly said. 'She *is* the best Cinderella.'

I looked at her in surprise. Someone needed to check her temperature. She was clearly unwell if she was making comments like that.

Khalila smiled and turned to Papà. 'Please, Mr Giorgi, will you let Valentina come back to ballet?'

Mamma began to translate, but Papà held up his hand to silence her. 'I understood her,' he said.

My heart was racing. Khalila was brave and had done what I'd been too scared to do. I braced myself for the answer, not sure if I was ready to hear it.

'What? Valentina's not dancing anymore?' One of the men, Enrico, shouted in Italian.

'Since when? That girl was born to dance,' another, Orazio, added.

I wasn't sure if their outburst would make things better or worse. Papà didn't like to look silly in front of anyone else. I studied his face. I didn't need to say anything. Everyone else was fighting my battle for me.

Finally, Papà spoke, returning to Italian. 'Valentina needed a break. She will return to ballet this week.'

'*Evviva!*' Caterina cheered.

'What did he say?' Amelia asked.

I contained my smile for a moment longer. 'He said he

would only allow me to return to ballet if you ate one of the pig feet.'

Khalila burst out laughing. Amelia looked horrified.

'It was a joke. You won. I can come back,' I said. I couldn't stop the smile from lighting up my face any longer. Everything felt right in the world again.

As if to celebrate, loud music suddenly cut through the crisp air. Orazio had pulled out his accordion and was playing a traditional tune. Caterina immediately jumped up onto her seat to dance, loving being the centre of attention. Everyone clapped their hands in time with the music and cheered her on. Before long, the tables had been pushed to the side and the sausage-making army was dancing across the grass.

'*Siete ballerine! Dovete ballare!*' Enrico called to Khalila, Amelia and me. The girls looked at me blankly.

'He said, "You are ballerinas, you need to dance!"' I translated. It was all the encouragement Khalila needed. Within seconds she had joined Caterina on the grass and was swinging her around.

'Well?' I said, holding my hand out to Amelia.

She laughed and tried to wave me away. 'I don't know how to dance to this!'

'It is easy! There are no rules!' I cried, tugging her into the crowd.

Amelia's whole body was stiff as she awkwardly swayed to the music.

'This is not ballet!' I yelled to her. 'You need to relax. No one here knows how to dance and no one cares. It is only for fun!' To prove my point, I cocked my head in the direction of Anna-Maria, who was dancing around as if she were trying to shake off a spider. I once again grabbed Amelia by the hand and spun her around. Finally she gave in, and before long we were dancing around in a circle with Khalila and Caterina, kicking our legs in time with the music and cheering along with the crowd. We danced and giggled until we were completely breathless.

'God, why isn't the Academy this fun?' Khalila said. She was jigging on the spot and waving her arms around in the air. It wasn't exactly the Tarantella, but it was close enough.

'The Academy *is* this fun!' I said with a grin. Although Khalila had a point. Today we were dancing without any pressure and it felt good. 'Well, it is when I am not making a mess of everything. I cannot wait to be back at rehearsal.'

'Miss Lily had better give you your role back,' Khalila said.

I stopped dancing. 'What? Do you think she will not?'

'Well, you've missed two weeks. We've learnt all of the choreography now,' Khalila said.

My heart sunk. I'd had my dream waved in front of my face and now there was a chance it was going to be snatched away again.

'Leave it to me,' Amelia said confidently.

21
Amelia

I must have lost my mind. It was the only possible explanation for what I'd just done. It was easy while we were dancing around and being silly to forget the consequences of what I was doing, but as I sat out the front of Valentina's house, waiting for Khalila's mum to pick us up, the panic started to set in. I'd been so caught up, that I had completely forgotten that helping Valentina meant ruining my own life.

For the past fortnight, I had been Cinderella. I had escaped from my lie, in fact, it had vanished completely. I had the perfect opportunity to avoid coming clean to my parents. I could have danced Cinderella, stolen the show, and they would have been none the wiser.

Instead, for the first time in my entire life, I put another dancer first. Well, kind of. I also did it because the Fairy Godmother's choreography was way better than Cinderella's, but that was just a minor detail. Now once again, I found myself stressing out about telling my parents the truth. How was I going to explain to them that I wasn't dancing the lead role as I'd so enthusiastically led them to believe, that instead, I was a supporting character.

Maybe I was better off faking an injury and pulling out of the show completely. That way my parents would remain completely oblivious. But if I did that, then I wouldn't get to dance as the Fairy Godmother. Mei-Lin would do it and make a horrible mess of everything. For someone who was usually a really good dancer, Mei-Lin was really struggling as the Fairy Godmother.

'You did good today, Milly.'

I looked up to see Khalila walking towards me. She had forgotten her phone and had raced back inside to get it.

'Thanks,' I muttered.

'Are you disappointed you won't be Cinderella anymore?' she asked, perching on the fence beside me.

I sighed. 'Yeah, I guess. Mum's gunna be a bit disappointed, that's all.'

'Nah, surely not. You're the Fairy Godmother and your dances are insane! She's gunna be blown away,' Khalila said, gazing out at the street.

'I dunno about that.'

'Plus, it's just the Academy's midyear show. It's not like you're dancing for The Australian Ballet or anything like that,' Khalila waved her hand loftily as she spoke.

I stared at her in shock. 'You don't take it seriously, do you? The Academy? It's performances like the midyear show that lead towards dancing for companies like The Australian Ballet. If you don't think they matter, why are you even bothering?' I asked.

'Woah, chill. You know there's more to life than ballet, right?'

Khalila didn't get it. Ballet was my entire life. Without that, I had nothing.

'Maybe for you,' I muttered.

'What? Just because I don't get the lead roles and I talk a lot at the studio, doesn't mean I don't love ballet. I wouldn't be at the Academy if I didn't. I just *love* everything about ballet and I want to *enjoy* everything about it. Vale and me, we don't have families like yours. Our families don't get ballet and we have to constantly prove ourselves so that *hopefully* one day they'll understand that it's not just a hobby. Your parents love ballet. You're so lucky.'

I stared down the street, avoiding looking at Khalila. She was right. I didn't have to fight to do ballet like some of the other kids did. That didn't mean I had it easy though.

'Maybe there's less pressure your way,' I said.

'Sometimes. Maybe. But I also think you're the main person putting pressure on yourself. You need to loosen up a bit. See the fun side of ballet. Anyway, just something to think about,' Khalila said, standing up as a silver SUV pulled up alongside the curb. 'And in all seriousness, it's really cool what you did for Vale and it was fun hanging out with you today. I even felt like the better dancer for once,' she teased, waving me towards her car.

'Ha! Don't get used to it.' I followed behind Khalila, returning her mum's smile as I climbed into the back seat. A week ago, I never would have expected to be hanging out with Khalila. In fact, I'd talked more at the Academy in the past week than I had since Alice left. It was kind of nice to be included in something for once. It made me nervous though. I was giving up a lead role, a chance to put myself in the spotlight. Had I lost focus of the end goal and what was really important?

22
Valentina

I crept up the Academy stairs, praying I wouldn't run into any of the other students. Amelia had convinced me to meet early so she could help me catch up on the choreography ahead of the evening's rehearsal. It had been a mad rush to get to the Academy straight from school. I had to start my homework in the car, which wasn't easy given Anna-Maria's driving.

There were a few mums milling around reception, drinking takeaway coffees and waiting for their kids to finish class. I could hear music and the loud voices of the Junior kids wafting out of Studio A. Thankfully that meant Miss Lily was preoccupied. I wasn't ready to face her yet. I made my way down the long corridor towards Studio C. It was the smallest of the three studios, often forgotten about because it was right up the back of the building and only had mirrors along one wall. It was too small to fit an entire class of students, and was usually only used for private lessons. For me, it was perfect. Being smaller, it felt safe.

I inched the door open and peered inside. I wasn't surprised to see Amelia already at the barre, warming up. She looked up as I entered the room. 'About time you got here,' she said.

'Sorry, I was as quick as I could be,' I said. It was true. If Anna-Maria had driven any faster, I would have needed a helmet.

I walked over to the barre and sat down to put my shoes on. I kneaded my thumbs into the arches of my feet, trying to warm them up a bit, before carefully pulling on each of my pointe shoes. I'd only had two weeks off, but based on the stiffness of my body, it felt like a month. I wasn't sure I was ready for a private lesson. Particularly, not one taught by Amelia. I eyed her suspiciously, trying to figure out what she was up to and why she would want to help me keep the role she so desperately wanted for herself.

'So, what are we actually doing here?' I asked.

'We're getting you ready to dance Cinderella,' Amelia said. She acted as if it was the most natural thing in the world, when in actual fact, it was completely crazy.

I stood up and began working my feet through my pointe shoes. I moved my ankles in circles, before slowly rolling each of my feet up and down in my shoes. 'But *why*? I don't understand. *Sei andata fuori di testa!*'

'What?'

'You have lost your mind. Or so it seems,' I explained. I was becoming more comfortable with my English, but some phrases still sounded better in Italian.

'Believe it or not, I like the Fairy Godmother better. Plus, I can't stand Ava and Kate and I don't want them to get what they want,' Amelia said, walking over to the speaker where her phone was plugged in. 'Now, the ball scene is where it really turns to poo. Miss Lily changed some things. First, show me what you know of the solo parts,' she said, pressing play on the music. She crossed her arms and waited for me to start.

My stomach churned at the sound of the familiar tune. Like lava erupting from a volcano, all of the emotions from my last rehearsal washed over me. I looked at the door, wondering if it was too late to run. I knew I wouldn't get far before Amelia caught me. I swallowed and took the first steps.

Amelia was watching me closely. I felt ridiculous dancing in front of her when I knew she could do a better job. I stumbled through the steps, struggling to concentrate on the choreography.

As I got to a *pirouette*, I relaxed into a *plié*, focused my eyes on a spot on the wall and in one swift motion, pushed off. It was as if someone had flicked a switch activating all of the muscles in my body. I gracefully landed the triple turn, before moving onto the next step.

The music suddenly stopped.

'I don't get it,' Amelia said.

I skidded to a halt and looked over at her. '*Cosa c'è?*'

'You're an absolute mess, then you do this perfect triple *pirouette* like it's the easiest thing in the world. How on earth does that work?' she said. She narrowed her eyes as if trying to read my mind.

I rubbed my lips together. They were dry from holding my breath. 'Um … I do not know … turns … they are easy. For me.'

It was the best I could come up with. Amelia was right though. It made no sense. Why was I finding the rest so hard? If I thought about the steps, they were easy. None of them were new. I'd danced much harder variations back home.

'Go again,' Amelia said. She restarted the music.

I took a deep breath and tried again. I must have looked like a complete idiot. I was trying my best, but I couldn't do anything right.

'Come on, Vale, concentrate. They're easy steps and you're making them look like work,' Amelia yelled over the music.

Her words blended into the chords of the piano. I pursed my lips and kept going. I did a series of quick *relevés* and faltered, forgetting what was next. Behind the music, I was forced to hurry to catch up. Out of the corner of my eye, I could see Amelia. Her arms were crossed and she looked completely fed up.

'Your eyes are unfocused and wandering all over the place. Concentrate! Wrong leg! Gosh, my baby cousin could do those steps and she doesn't even know how to walk yet. Sloppy fingers! *Focus!*'

Tension prickled through my body. I couldn't hear words, only yelling. It was so distracting. I pursed my lips even tighter and willed myself to remember.

'Shoulders down! They're all the way up by your ears. You're racing the music. Slow down! *Listen*. Stretch your legs!'

I felt like my head was about to explode. I jolted to a sudden stop and clenched my fists. A low growl escaped my lips. '*Basta!* Enough! I cannot do this!'

Amelia paused the music. 'What do you mean you *cannot* do this? Do you want to be Cinderella or not?' She stared at me, her bright blue eyes blazing.

'I cannot do this with you, in the room, yelling. I cannot understand English when I dance so it is just angry noise and it is very distracting. You said you were going to help me.'

'I am helping you,' Amelia snapped.

'No, you are not. I feel this big,' I said. I held up my hand with my index finger and thumb slightly apart. 'I feel stupid when you watch me. Stupid for not understanding and then when I try to translate, I forget what I am doing. I know you can dance Cinderella easily. It is embarrassing. I got the role but you are so much better than me.'

At the end of my outburst, I turned my back to Amelia and rested my hands on my head. I closed my eyes and took a deep breath to try and calm myself.

'There's your problem. Right there.'

I turned back around to face Amelia.

She was pointing her finger directly at me. '*Suck. It. Up.* This is a ballet school. If you're scared of competition, choose another hobby. So you don't understand the corrections? Tell Miss Lily that, then don't worry about them while you're dancing and ask what they were once the music has stopped. If you spend your whole time thinking you can't be Cinderella, well then, it's not going to work. You might as well give up now. Go play soccer or something,' Amelia said with a flick of her hand.

I leant against the ballet barre to steady myself. Amelia was right. I just didn't know how to switch my mind off so I could dance without worrying about what other people thought of me. It was in my DNA to worry about the opinions of other people. *Fare la bella figura.* It was my family's favourite motto. 'So, what am I supposed to do?' I asked flatly.

'Get over yourself. There are enough people at a ballet school to tell you what you're doing wrong, you don't need to beat yourself up too. Haven't you realised, the more you doubt yourself, the worse you get?' Amelia said. Her voice was strained with frustration. 'Your *pirouettes* are awesome because you trust yourself when you do them. You need to be like that with the rest of the steps. Pretend you're dancing in your backyard with no one watching. Miss Lily chose you at the audition. When you dance properly, you dance with your heart. You lose yourself in the dance. It's beautiful to watch.'

I smiled. It was the nicest thing Amelia had ever said to me. Perhaps the nicest thing anyone had ever said. If Khalila were here, she'd probably have a heart attack.

'Now think about that and do it again. Push everything else out of your mind. All you need to think about is the steps – where your feet need to go, whether you're standing up straight and holding your stomach tight. The rest is just background noise,' Amelia ordered.

'And you will not yell at me?'

Amelia sighed. 'I won't yell at you. Now hurry up! We don't have all day!'

'You are very bossy, you know,' I said.

I lifted my arms into position and waited for the music to start. When the chords sounded out from the speakers,

I did exactly as Amelia had told me to. It felt like I was learning the dance all over again. I concentrated on the feeling of the wooden floor beneath my toes and the strain of my arches as I pointed my feet. I felt a burst of energy ripple along my arms, all the way to my fingertips. Every time doubt crept into my mind, I shoved it back out again. *Background noise*, that's what Amelia had called it. I tuned into the music and let myself be transformed into Cinderella. When the music finally came to an end, I was exhausted. I flopped both arms over my head and walked in slow circles, trying to catch my breath.

'You messed up the ending completely,' Amelia said.

My heart sank. I really thought the dance had felt good.

'But the rest of the dance was much better. It was like watching someone else,' Amelia said.

I grinned. Was it really that easy? I never would have guessed that all this time, part of me had been sabotaging myself.

'You still have a lot of work to do, but you can do it in rehearsal. Coming?' Amelia said, heading towards the door.

I drew in my breath sharply, then marched after her.

I was warming up at the barre when in the reflection of the mirror, I saw Kate and Ava walk into the studio. My grip on the wood tightened. I now knew what Khalila had meant all those weeks ago when she had said the two of them were trouble. I pretended not to notice them, continuing my warm-up.

'Valentina, you came back,' Kate gushed, leaning against the barre beside me.

I kept my eyes down, following my foot as it slid across the floor, pointing to the front, side and then behind me.

'It's a shame you took so long though. Miss Lily had to replace you,' Ava said. 'We thought you made a really good Cinderella.'

I stopped mid-exercise. Was this Aussie sarcasm again? There was no way they thought I was a good Cinderella.

'Vale, can you help me stretch?' Khalila said. She grabbed my arm and pulled me away. 'Ignore them,' she muttered under her breath.

With a loud clap, Miss Lily appeared in the studio. My heart skipped a beat.

'Okay everyone, it's crunch time! Next week we are on stage. This week is our final chance to iron out any creases,' Miss Lily paused for a moment as her eyes locked with mine. 'At this point in time, I shouldn't be seeing any major red flags.'

Was I a red flag? I didn't know what I was supposed to do. Should I raise my hand and ask whether I could still be Cinderella, or hang to the side and wait for Miss Lily to notice me?

'Miss Giorgi, it's nice of you to finally rejoin us. I trust you have a good explanation for your extended holiday?'

'I …' I didn't know what to say.

'Valentina's been rehearsing with me to make sure she's up to date,' Amelia said.

Miss Lily looked surprised. 'That's … surprising. Well, I'm impressed you stepped up, Amelia. Okay, enough time wasting. Opening positions, Act Two, Scene One,' Miss Lily said as she plugged in the iPad.

I couldn't believe my luck. Was it really that simple? I grinned at Amelia as I made my way to my opening position.

'You're kidding right?' Ava suddenly said.

Miss Lily's hand hovered over the iPad. 'Is there a problem, Ava?'

'Well, we've all been working our butts off and Valentina hasn't been here at all. It's not fair for her to play Cinderella,' she said, glaring at me as she spoke.

My stomach dropped. So much for Ava being happy for me. I didn't know why she cared so much. It didn't affect her role at all.

'Does anyone else feel that way?' Miss Lily asked, turning to face the class.

Kate's hand shot into the air. Mei-Lin hesitated, before raising hers too, mouthing *sorry* to me as she did.

'In the interest of being fair, we'll have a vote. All those in favour of Valentina playing Cinderella, raise your hands,' Miss Lily instructed. She glanced around the room.

Amelia, Khalila, Sam and Liam all raised their hands, along with some of the other dancers.

'And those against?' Miss Lily said.

I watched as the rest of the students raised their hands. My stomach swarmed. I was so close to getting what I wanted. The thought of it being taken away again made me feel sick.

Miss Lily counted the hands. 'It's a tie,' she announced.

'So, what happens now?' Sam asked.

'I don't have time for this,' Miss Lily said, rubbing her temples.

'Miss Lily, can I say something?' Amelia said, raising her hand. Miss Lily nodded for her to go on. 'Given it's a tie and I'm currently filling in for Vale, can't I make the call that I'm happy for her to dance Cinderella instead of me?'

Miss Lily folded her arms and looked between Amelia and me. 'And you're actually happy to step down?' she asked in surprise.

Amelia nodded.

'Well then I guess –' Miss Lily began.

'But that's not fair *either*!' Mei-Lin whined. 'If Amelia goes back to playing the Fairy Godmother, I'm back in the *corps*. *All* because of Valentina!'

'Give me strength,' Miss Lily muttered under her breath with a long sigh.

I bit my lip. Perhaps it had been a bad idea coming back to the Academy after all. All I seemed to do was cause trouble.

'That's ridiculous!' Amelia cried. 'Miss Lily, you always tell us ballet's a tough industry and we need to act like professionals. Well, in a *professional* company, wouldn't an understudy only get to perform the role if the lead dancer was injured, or doing a terrible job?' Amelia asked.

'Which she *clearly* was,' Ava muttered to Kate.

I watched on helplessly. Once again, Amelia was fighting my battle for me and I was at a complete loss for words and unable to help.

'Miss Lily, if you want us to understand how a professional company works, then we need to be treated like professionals. It doesn't matter if someone's new, if they're the best person for the role, then so be it,' Amelia smiled at Khalila as if sharing a secret. 'Given we're all here, casting should stay with how you originally wanted it,' Amelia said.

I held my breath. My fingers were crossed behind my back.

Miss Lily took another deep breath. 'Amelia has a valid point and we're wasting far too much time. Time we don't have. Original casting stands, but Valentina, you've got one chance. Prove to me you're the right person to dance Cinderella, or you're out. Opening positions of the *pas de deux*. Now!'

Of course she'd picked the scene I was most uncomfortable with. I dried my sweaty palms against my ballet tights and glanced across at Sam. He smiled encouragingly. It was now or never.

'You've got this,' Khalila said as she walked to her position.

I smiled nervously. 'Thank you,' I whispered as I passed Amelia.

'Don't thank me yet. Just don't stuff it up,' she replied.

I let out a small laugh. Some parts of Amelia hadn't changed at all. I watched as she walked over to Miss Lily and whispered something in her ear. Miss Lily glanced over at me, then nodded at Amelia. I furrowed my brow. What was going on now?

As I waited for the music to start, I took a deep breath and closed my eyes. I thought back to my little school in the Old Town. Instead of thinking about how much I missed it, I thought about how much it had taught me. The *pirouettes* I'd perfected, the way Maestra Anna had insisted that every tiny step be precise, and that our movements carry all the way through to our fingertips.

When I opened my eyes, I saw Kate and Ava watching with smug expressions on their faces. They wanted me to fail and they were going to be sadly disappointed. A spark of energy rippled through my body. If I wanted to play Cinderella, then I would. It was up to me to prove myself. I smiled confidently at Ava and Kate, feeling like myself for the first time in weeks.

As the music started, it was as if everyone else in the room had vanished. I was Cinderella preparing to dance with the Prince. My feet glossed over the ground, barely making a sound. I felt Cinderella's excitement and nerves over doing something no one wanted her to do.

Sam held out his hand and winked as I took it. Any fear I had of dancing with a boy had completely vanished. I let Sam guide me around the room. With his help, my turns were faster and my leaps were higher. I felt lighter than a feather. I stepped towards Sam for the fish dive lift and for the first time, I didn't feel scared. I felt excited.

In one swift motion, Sam lifted me off the floor and tilted me downwards. I grinned up at him as we waited for the music to finish. As Sam placed me back on the ground, I realised my classmates were clapping. Khalila, of course, the loudest of them all. I glanced over at Kate and Ava.

They both had sour looks on their faces. I winked at them.

'I told you you could do it,' Khalila whispered, sidling up beside me.

'Thank you, I just hope it was enough,' I said. I looked hopefully across at Miss Lily, realising that she hadn't called out a single correction during my dance. Had it been perfect or had Amelia let Miss Lily in on my secret?

Miss Lily tapped the side of her glasses in thought. The suspense was killing me. Finally, she spoke.

'Cinderella … it's good to have you back,' she said with a smile.

23
Amelia

The scent of hairspray and well-loved dance shoes filled the air, giving me goosebumps. If someone made a perfume and called the fragrance 'Show Time', that's exactly what it would smell like. My hair was completely plastered down, yet I still felt the need to spray it one more time to make sure no wispy strands could escape as I danced.

Opening night had come around quickly. Too quickly. The past week felt like a complete blur, chock-a-block full of rehearsals at the Academy and at the theatre. I had to give Valentina credit; she had barely stopped dancing since her return. Whenever the other students were taking a break, I'd see Valentina in a corner somewhere, practising her choreography and polishing it to perfection. As a group, we were ready to perform, but for the first time ever, it was me who didn't feel ready.

I glanced around the dressing-room. Around me, dancers were doing their makeup, putting on costumes or stretching. It made me think of Mum's dressing-room when I was just a tiny tot. I'd sit in the corner, eagerly watching the professional ballerinas apply their makeup and put on their costumes. It was like magic. They would transform into princesses, fairies, dolls ... whatever the ballet called for. It was in those dressing-rooms that I had decided I wanted to be a ballerina too. I'd do my best to copy the dancers as they ran through their routines, desperately hoping someone would notice how talented I was and let me go onstage too.

When the West Australian Ballet performed *Cinderella*, my dream came true. Kind of. I was six years old and got to dress as a fairy and sit beside Cinderella in the coach as she travelled across the stage to the ball. Of course, Mum was Cinderella. She had been good enough to get the lead. I sighed as I painted foundation across my face. It was impossible to be fully excited about the performance when there was a ticking time bomb on the verge of an explosion. *The lie.*

Beside me, Valentina was quietly styling her hair into a bun. I watched her face in the mirror. Her lips were pursed tightly together as she dragged her brush through her thick, wavy brown hair. She wrestled it into a ponytail at the crown of her head, ready to be secured with an elastic band. As she stretched the elastic around her pony, a chunk of hair sprung from her grip. She growled in frustration and let go of the rest.

'You okay?' I asked.

Valentina locked eyes with me in the mirror. 'I do my hair every single day without any problem. But today, I am shaking so much it is not working. I am just so nervous.'

'Pull yourself together,' I said. 'You're going to psych yourself out again.'

'Psych? Ah, *ho capito*. I know. I am just stressing out about my family seeing me dance.'

She wasn't the only one. At least her family weren't in for any nasty surprises. The minute the curtain went up, my parents would get the shock of their lives. No doubt they would spend Act One trying to figure out why the casting was wrong. I couldn't believe I'd made it all the way to opening night without my mum finding out the truth. If it weren't such a disaster, it would actually be quite funny.

My hand shook as I dusted eye shadow across my lids. I couldn't let Valentina or any of the other dancers see how nervous I was. They'd think I had stage fright and that couldn't be any further from the truth.

For awhile, Valentina and I worked in silence, busy transforming ourselves into something we weren't. As I finished applying the final coat of mascara, I leant towards the mirror to examine my work. My big blue eyes stared back at me. I didn't look like me and lately, I hadn't felt like me either. I didn't know who this new Amelia was – the one who lied and lost focus helping other dancers.

'Do you know where Khalila is?' Valentina asked, breaking into my thoughts.

I shook my head. 'Probably flapping around with the baby birds.' I applied a coat of lipstick, smacking my lips together to finish.

'Is your family here tonight, too?' Valentina asked.

I walked away from the mirror to stretch. I really didn't like making small talk before a performance. I preferred to stay quiet and focused. 'Yep. Mum and Dad,' I said. *And André.* Mum had already sent a message saying he'd arrived at the theatre and was excited to see me perform. My stomach churned.

'You are lucky, you know,' Valentina said.

Here we go again with the luck. It was so easy for everyone else to say when they really had no idea. I stayed quiet, stretching out into a low lunge.

'None of my family understands ballet,' Valentina continued. 'Back home, in my town, girls only dance when they are small. No one really takes it seriously. I hope after tonight, Papà will understand more.'

I nodded quietly. There was nothing really to say. I stood up and extended my leg up into a mount, pulling my foot towards my head. As I did, I tried to focus on the pull through my hamstring, rather than the nerves that were tugging at my stomach. I'd never been more nervous before a performance and it was all because of that stupid lie. I really should have taken Valentina's part when I'd had the chance. It would have solved all of my problems and André would have left the theatre impressed.

'Nice of you to show up tonight, Valentina.'

I tilted my head to see Kate and Ava strutting through the change room. They were already in costume, dressed up as the Stepsisters. Kate had a yellow satin dress, while Ava had a bright orange one. The colour choice was a bit unfortunate for Ava given her fire engine red hair. The combo made her look like she had burst into flames.

'Of course I am here,' Valentina said, her eyebrows crinkling in confusion.

'Well, you skipped enough rehearsals, we half expected you to skip the performance too,' Kate said with a smirk.

'Or are you waiting for your dad to drag you offstage during the first act?' Ava asked.

I studied Valentina. She seemed to shrink in size each time Kate or Ava spoke. She opened her mouth to respond, but then closed it, as if changing her mind.

'Haven't you two got anything better to do? Stuffing a bra or something?' I said, lowering my leg. Kate and Ava glared at me, before leaving the room. I'd become way too involved in dance drama lately.

Valentina smiled gratefully, but her eyes still looked sad. As much trouble as I was going to be in over my lie, I knew there was no way I could have taken Valentina's role. I was starting to think she needed it more than I did. I'd just have to brace myself to face the music.

'Dancers, this is your ten-minute call!'

My breath caught in my throat as the announcement came through the dressing-room speakers.

'Ten minutes. I repeat, dancers, this is your ten-minute call.'

Ten minutes until the curtain would rise. Ten minutes until everyone found out I was a big, fat liar. Sometimes, ten minutes felt like a really long time, like if you were at school and waiting for recess. Ten minutes seemed like forever then. But ten minutes wasn't very long at all if you were about to ruin your life.

'Ten minutes,' Valentina shrieked as she finished doing up the back of her dress. '*Oh dio,* can you believe it? I have never been so nervous in my life! Not even once. Have you?'

I couldn't breathe. I shook my head, blankly staring at myself in the mirror.

'Amelia? Are you okay?' Valentina asked, pausing as she headed towards the dressing-room door. 'You look like you have seen *un fantasma* … a ghost.'

I forced a smile. 'I'm fine. I just need a moment.'

Valentina frowned. 'I can wait?'

I shook my head and waved her out of the room. Right now, I needed to be alone.

Valentina hesitated for a moment, before stepping out into the hallway. 'Okay, but do not be long. I'm going backstage to do some stretching. See you there!'

As soon as she had gone, I grabbed my dance jacket and loosely wrapped it around my shoulders. I made my way out of the dressing-room, but instead of heading towards the stage, I made a beeline for the exit.

24
Valentina

From the wings at the side of the stage, I could just make out the audience. I'd been told the auditorium was completely full. Not a single spare seat in the entire theatre. Somewhere amongst the crowd were my parents, waiting to see me perform. Not just my parents, the entire Italian community of Perth. Mamma had invited pretty much everyone we'd met since moving to Australia. My stomach swarmed with butterflies. It was a lot of pressure, performing for all of those people, but the one person who made me most nervous of all was Papà. I was desperate to prove myself to him. I loved ballet and needed him to see that it was much more than just a hobby. That for me, it was just as important as family, food and tradition.

'Five minutes. Dancers, this is your five-minute call.'

My stomach did a flip. I inhaled and smiled, letting the tension melt out of my body. In just five minutes I would become Cinderella and finally, I felt ready.

'Vale, you look amazing!'

I turned to see Khalila. At least, I thought it was Khalila. Her face was hidden behind the most incredible makeup I had ever seen. A small, pointy prosthetic beak covered her nose, and the rest of her face had been painted green with specks of glitter around her eyes. She even had giant wings attached to her arms and a feathered crown. I wasn't a great lover of birds, but Khalila looked fantastic. 'Wow, Khalila! You look ... wow! That makeup is *magnifico!*'

'Hey, have you seen Amelia? Miss Lily was looking for her but I can't find her anywhere,' Khalila said, the hint of a frown visible behind her beak.

'What do you mean you cannot find her anywhere? She was in the dressing-room with me, and she said she would meet me here. You did not pass her in the corridor?' I asked.

Khalila shook her head. 'There are less than five minutes to go. No way Amelia wouldn't be backstage by now.'

'Did I just hear someone say Amelia's not backstage?' Miss Lily called from her position behind the stage manager's desk. She lifted up her glasses and craned her neck, her eyes searching through the sea of dancers backstage.

'I have no idea where she is. Most of the dressing-rooms were empty when I came back here,' Khalila said with a frown.

'Why are my dancers trying to send me into early retirement this year?' Miss Lily murmured. 'Can someone find Amelia, please?' she called out to the backstage crew.

'I'll find her, Miss Lily. I'm not on until she is. She's probably just on the loo or something,' Khalila said.

We exchanged a glance. Neither of us believed that one bit. I had a bad feeling about Amelia's disappearance. She hadn't seemed herself when I had left her in the dressing-room. I felt a pang of guilt. After everything Amelia had done for me, I should have double-checked she was okay.

'One minute, dancers. Cinderella, please take your place,' the stage manager waved me towards the stage. I looked frantically back at Khalila.

'Go, it's fine. I'll find her. Honestly, it's Amelia. She'll be here somewhere. She's probably telling off one of the younger kids. Just get out there and perform your bum off, Cindy!' Khalila said, disappearing down the stairs towards the dressing-rooms.

I silently made my way onto the dimly lit stage. The curtain was still closed and I could see the shadows of the stage hands, quickly making their final adjustments to the set. By the time I found my position, they had disappeared. I was all alone, nervously waiting for the curtain to rise.

The soft hum of the audience began to die down, replaced instead by the strong beating of my heart. I felt like every noise was a million times louder. The audience could probably hear me breathing nervously.

The agonising seconds before the lights came up and the music began felt like hours. My stomach ached. I said a quick prayer that I would remember all of my choreography. Nonna probably wouldn't approve of a prayer like that. She would say it was selfish and a waste. For me though, this performance was bigger than the entire world. My eyebrow twitched. I wanted to scratch it, but I didn't dare in case the curtain opened.

I said another quick prayer that Khalila had found Amelia by now and that the two of them were busy stretching in the dark backstage. I couldn't understand how she could just vanish. Amelia lived for the stage. There had to be some sort of mistake. Maybe Khalila was right. Maybe she'd just gone to the toilet.

All thoughts of Amelia were snatched from my mind as the opening chords began to play. I took a deep breath and smiled as the curtain rose and the lights came up, revealing Cinderella's house.

25
Amelia

I slumped against the toilet cubical door. I felt sick and sorry for myself. I had spent the past five minutes vomiting and I could only put it down to my body being overwhelmed by panic.

I thought I'd be strong enough to go out onstage and deal with the consequences of my lie later, but I just couldn't do it. My parents, André, everyone would think I was a complete loser when they found out what I'd done. I wished I'd just told Mum the truth from the start. Instead, I had let the lie grow bigger and bigger until there was no way of undoing it. The worst part was I actually really loved being the Fairy Godmother. That didn't matter though because it wasn't the lead role. I hadn't been good enough to be cast as that. No one watched *Cinderella* and walked away talking about the Fairy Godmother. They only cared about Cinderella and the Prince.

I heard the opening chords of Act One. I pictured my parents sitting in the audience, confused and wondering why their daughter wasn't onstage. I needed to get far away from the theatre. Fast.

I flushed the toilet and made my way out of the stall. I was washing my hands when the bathroom door flew open. I froze. Georgie from the Junior ballet waltzed into the bathroom. She was dressed as a little blue bird and was humming a tune. Her face lit up when she saw me. 'Amelia! Wow! You look so beautiful!'

No one was supposed to see me. I was meant to be escaping. 'Georgie, what are you doing in here?'

Georgie gingerly reached out and touched one of the rhinestones on my tutu, her mouth forming a round O. She was at a complete loss for words.

'Georgie?'

'Your costume is the prettiest thing I've ever seen. I saw you dance the other day in rehearsal and when I got home, I told Mum that when I'm older I want to be the Fairy Godmother, just like you,' Georgie said proudly.

I smiled. 'I think you'd do a great job,' I said.

Georgie beamed up at me. 'Really? I'd love to fly around the stage, dancing on my toes. But I don't want blisters. I heard dancing on your toes makes your feet bleed. Do your feet bleed?' She stopped talking suddenly, then said, 'Everyone's looking for you, you know?'

I hesitated. As much as I wanted to push past Georgie and

make a run for it, I knew I couldn't. How could I leave when there were little kids who were actually excited to see me dance? I looked down at Georgie, who had reached out to touch another rhinestone. I twisted my lips in contemplation, then said, 'I'm on my way backstage right now.'

The bathroom door burst open. 'Oh my god, there you are!' Khalila said.

'I'm coming, I'm coming,' I said, rushing towards the door. 'See you onstage, Georgie!'

'Geez you gave everyone a heart attack,' Khalila said as we rushed down the corridor towards the stage. 'Quick, move your bony bum!'

As we pushed open the stage door, I shoved the thought of my angry parents out of my mind. I was back to my original plan. I'd deal with Mum and Dad later. For now, I had a job to do and I wanted to make sure I did it properly, for kids like Georgie who thought the Fairy Godmother was the coolest thing ever.

I silently crept through the shadows backstage. Loud music pulsed through my chest, my pounding heart adding to the symphony. I was relieved to see I still had a few minutes until it was my turn to go onstage. I took a few deep breaths to calm my nerves and began rising up and down in my pointe shoes to warm my feet back up. I cursed myself for wasting valuable time in the bathroom.

'Psst ... Milly,' Khalila hissed.

I held a finger up to my lips. You weren't allowed to talk backstage while the performance was on.

Unsurprisingly, Khalila ignored me. 'I just heard Ava fell over onstage before. She and Kate were doing their Stepsister dance and Kate accidentally tripped her over. Apparently, it looked like part of the show. Lucky, huh?' Khalila said, giggling.

One of the stagehands made an angry shushing noise. Khalila mouthed *sorry* in response.

I was secretly happy that Ava had fallen over onstage, but it would be bad luck to say so before I had danced myself. Knowing my luck, I'd be struck down by karma and end up falling on my bum, too. If the Fairy Godmother fell over, there was no way anyone would think it was part of the performance.

'Ava's so angry at Kate,' Khalila whispered, forgetting about the no-talking rule. 'Like, apparently, a vein in her forehead looked like it was about to burst.'

I tried my best to ignore her, focusing my attention on Valentina, who was currently dancing one of Cinderella's solos. From what I could see, she was doing a great job. She looked like her old self, the one from the audition who hadn't been tormented by Kate and Ava.

I needed to get my head in the zone. All the way back on

Valentina's first day, Miss Lily had said she couldn't wait to see the two of us onstage together, that we'd be a force to be reckoned with. I didn't want to disappoint her. One by one, I gently cracked my knuckles. It was one of my performance rituals. Mum hated me doing it.

Khalila was still chatting away next to me. 'Milly? Milly, did you hear me?' she hissed.

I whipped my head around to face Khalila. 'Will you *shut up*. I'm trying to focus.'

The stagehand shushed us once again. Everyone knew backstage was a quiet zone. Everyone but Khalila it seemed.

'Sorry,' she said sheepishly.

Once I'd finished cracking my knuckles, I shook my hands and jiggled my shoulders around. As I did, I felt some of the nervous energy leave my body. I looked down at my hands. Something was missing. 'My wand!' I hissed.

I pushed past Khalila and darted over to the prop table. The music in the background was changing. It was almost my cue. My eyes anxiously scanned the prop table in search of my wand. There was a bit of everything. Cinderella's tiara, a diamante-covered pointe shoe for the glass slipper, a bucket and sponge. Finally, my eyes landed on the wand. I snatched it up and raced back to my spot in the wings, just in time to go onstage.

I plastered on my stage smile and glided out of the wings, gently extending my wand up into the air. The lights on the stage were dim and the audience was coated in black. I couldn't see a single face. Just the way I liked it. Instead, I could see Valentina, curled in a heap at the front of the stage. Cinderella had just had her dress ripped by the Stepsisters as they left for the ball. She was in tears, clutching her torn dress, unaware of the magic unfolding behind her.

As I floated across the stage, I smiled softly. For the first time in what felt like forever, my smile was genuine. Being onstage was what I lived for. I could feel my excitement bringing my muscles to life. I didn't think about my parents or André, who were no doubt sitting in the audience with their jaws on the floor. Instead, I thought of Georgie, who wasn't so different to how I had been as a child. In all of the hype of the previous weeks I had completely forgotten what it had felt like when I had watched the Fairy Godmother dance for the very first time. The ballerina's feet had barely touched the ground. I had been certain she was flying. In that one moment, I believed magic really did exist. I wanted the audience to feel that way as they watched me.

As I reached Valentina's side, I gently tapped her on the shoulder with my wand. It might have been Valentina who lifted her head, but it was Cinderella I saw staring up at me. I grinned at her, before dancing back across the stage. I swished my leg up off the ground into a *grand jeté en tournant*. The jump was always impressive. At the peak of it, I changed legs in the air, before coming down to land. I danced back over to Valentina and reached for her hand. She smiled and let me help her to her feet.

Together, we glided around the stage, moving in perfect unison for the first time. As we reached centre stage, I theatrically circled the wand over my head. On cue, the birds ran out onto the stage, the older dancers leading the way for the Juniors.

My smile broadened as I heard the audience let out a breath of amazement. The birds circled around us, flapping the wings of their costumes in time with the music. Amongst them, Georgie grinned up at me. I knew the look. She was completely mesmerised by the magic.

I broke through the circle with a series of quick jumps. We had arrived at the most stressful time of the ballet. For Valentina, anyway. As the older birds and I distracted the audience with *grand jetés* and quick turns, the Junior birds ushered her off the stage so she could quickly get changed for the ball.

As I began my turns, I knew Valentina would be frantically changing her costume backstage, desperate to make it back in time for her cue. It was a tight window. She had precisely forty-seven seconds to change into a glittery tutu, tiara and diamante-covered pointe shoes. It was the pointe shoes that took the longest to tie up, but Valentina would have dressing assistants positioning her tiara and doing up her costume, leaving her to focus on her shoes.

I pushed Valentina out of mind, turning my focus back to the task at hand. I did a complicated combination of turns and jumps, my feet barely touching the ground in between each step. I was flying! I finished the sequence with a perfect triple *pirouette – finally!* As I came to a stop, I opened my arms up to the audience and was met with a thunderous round of applause.

I smiled and waved my wand towards the back corner of the stage, holding my breath. *Come on, Valentina.* As if by magic, Valentina burst out of the wings.

Cinderella was ready for the ball.

26
Valentina

A wave of relief washed over me as applause filled the theatre. I'd done it. I stood like a statue as the curtain closed for intermission, but the second it hit the ground, I spun around to find Khalila.

Act One had been a complete blur. The entire time it felt as if I was floating through a dream. It couldn't have been more perfect. My eyes finally landed on Khalila. I raced towards her and threw out my arms. 'That ... was incredible!' I said breathlessly.

Khalila returned my hug. 'And to think you almost gave up being Cinderella.'

I grinned sheepishly. Somewhere in the audience, my whole family had just seen me dance the best performance of my life. More than anything I hoped Papà was proud.

We chatted happily as we made our way back to the dressing-room to prepare for the second half of the ballet. We had twenty minutes to kill before we would return to the stage, but now that we'd shaken off our nerves, we could just enjoy ourselves. We found Amelia sitting on the floor of the dressing-room, carefully taking her shoes off. She winced at the sight of a new blister on her little toe.

'*Ahia!* That looks painful. Do you want a … *cerotto*? Sorry, I do not know the word,' I asked, pulling a box of Band-Aids out of my dance bag to show Amelia. She nodded, before carefully examining her other toes.

I plonked down on the floor beside her and passed over the Band-Aid. 'You were incredible out there. I was watching the audience as you came onstage. It was like they were … hypnotised.'

Amelia wrapped the Band-Aid around her toe, before massaging the arches of her feet. 'Thanks,' she said, not looking up.

'But way to send the whole theatre into a tizz pre-show. What the heck were you doing?' Khalila asked. She was sprawled on her back across the dressing-room floor, her bird wings spread out around her.

Amelia shrugged. 'You worried over nothing. The Fairy Godmother wasn't in the first scene. There was no point being backstage waiting around with all you other clowns. I needed the bathroom. I knew I wasn't gunna be late.'

'*Right* … so little Miss Prima Ballerina makes her own rules now?' Khalila said, raising her eyebrow. 'Ballet's newest rebel. I don't buy it.'

I chuckled. It was hard to take Khalila seriously when she was still dressed up as a bird. I didn't believe Amelia either, but everything had turned out fine, so there was no point worrying about it now.

Khalila let out a small growl, stamping her feet against the carpet. Her eyes were scrunched close and her beak was twitching.

'What are you doing *now*?' Amelia asked dryly.

'Are you okay, little bird?' I asked. I leant in closer to Khalila and studied her face.

She sniffed, her beak wiggling up and down as she opened and closed her mouth. 'I have the worst itch … on my nose … but it's underneath my beak and I'm not allowed to touch any of my makeup. Miss Lily's rules after Mya accidentally knocked her beak off pre-show.'

I giggled. Amelia rolled her eyes.

'Amelia Rose, do you want to tell me what's going on, or am I expected to guess?'

We all fell silent. Amelia's mum was standing at the dressing-room door. Her eyebrows were raised in the same angry arch that Amelia was so well known for.

I glanced at Khalila, who sat up and pulled a face.

Between us, Amelia's cheeks had turned rosy red.

27
Amelia

I'd never moved faster in my life. At the sight of Mum, I scrambled to my feet, grabbed my dance jacket and raced for the door. 'Mum, can we go for a walk?'

I knew exactly what was coming, I just didn't know how bad it was going to be. I needed to get Mum as far away from everyone else as possible before she made a scene.

'I think that's a very good idea,' Mum replied, leaving the room. Her voice sounded light, but I knew that would change as soon as we were clear of the dressing-room. I avoided Valentina's and Khalila's enquiring eyes as I headed out the door.

'Everything is okay?' Valentina called after me.

I waved her off and left the room. Mum was already at the other end of the corridor. I scurried to catch up. It had been years since she'd retired from dancing professionally, but she still had the air of a ballerina. She was wafer thin, had perfect posture and seemed to glide as she walked. And boy, did she walk quickly. Though the majority of the time she was calm and composed, when she got angry, she was terrifying.

'Mum, I can explain,' I said, doing my best to catch up.

As I reached the end of the corridor, Mum pivoted around to face me. 'Imagine my surprise when your dad and I were sitting in the audience, next to André might I add, waiting for you to appear as Cinderella, but instead, the curtain opens to reveal Valentina. What happened? Did you lose the part?'

I bit my lip. There was no easy way of explaining what had happened. Even I didn't really understand everything that had unfolded in the past few weeks. 'No ... not exactly,' I said. I paused, carefully choosing my words. 'Well ...Valentina got the role to start with and I was cast as the Fairy Godmother. But I didn't know how to tell you when you asked, so ... so I said I was the lead.'

'Amelia!'

'I know, it was a really bad thing to do. But I was so embarrassed and I knew you'd be disappointed.'

'Disappointed? And you thought I'd be more impressed if you lied about it instead?'

'Yes ... no ... well, it was an accident. It just came out.' The conversation was making me sweat even more than I had while dancing under the hot stage lights. 'I was going to tell you, honest, but every time I tried you were just so excited and I couldn't get a word in. Then you invited André. Everything got completely out of hand. Then Valentina didn't do so well in rehearsals and her parents pulled her out of class, so I got to step in as Cinderella.'

Mum narrowed her eyes. I felt like she could see right through me sometimes. I wished I had the same power. I didn't know whether my explanation was helping or not.

'But Valentina's a great dancer and the reason she wasn't doing well was because she was stressed about her family and she couldn't understand Miss Lily's English ... because she's Italian, remember?'

Mum nodded.

'And then to make matters worse, some of the other girls were saying really nasty things about her.'

'You better not have been one of them,' Mum said sternly.

I groaned. 'Mum! Will you just listen to me?' I exclaimed in frustration.

Mum pursed her lips. I grimaced. I had to keep my cool. I couldn't afford to make Mum angrier than she already was. 'Sorry!' I quickly corrected myself. 'Of course I wasn't one of the girls being mean. You know I keep to myself at ballet. But then I felt sorry for Valentina, so I ended up helping her get her role back. Plus, the Fairy Godmother's choreography was way better than Cinderella's. That's what I was doing when you found me in the garage studio.'

Mum crossed her arms and leant back against the wall. She didn't say a word. Her silence only made me more nervous. I studied her face, trying to figure out what she was thinking. She had the best poker face in the world. I glanced at the clock in the corridor. Intermission was running out. I wished Mum would just hurry up and yell at me so I could go back to the dressing-room and finish getting ready for Act Two.

'What I don't understand is why you didn't just tell me the truth to begin with?'

'Because ... I was embarrassed,' I said. It was even more embarrassing to admit out loud. 'I work so hard all the time and I do so many extra private lessons. I should have been the lead.'

Mum placed one hand on my shoulder, and with the other tilted my chin up to look her in the eyes. 'There's nothing embarrassing about being cast as the Fairy Godmother. I've danced it myself, more than once,' she said. 'You need to be grateful for any role you get, even if it's not your first preference. Ballet is competitive, I thought I'd taught you that. You need to be resilient and learn from every experience and use it to grow. Plus, you make a fabulous Fairy Godmother!'

I felt like the biggest idiot on the planet. Of course that was Mum's response to the casting. I should have expected it all along.

'As for helping Valentina, well, I'm proud of you. Ballet is just as much about friendship as it is about dance. It's a lonely life if you don't share it with the people around you. I'm not saying don't be competitive, you need to push yourself, but you also need to understand that it takes an entire team to put together a ballet production. It comes together much better if you're all working together towards the same goal. Your dad and I have been trying to teach you that for years.'

'What about André? He must think I'm pretty unprofessional, huh?'

'Well, he was confused, that's for sure. I told him he must have got his wires crossed, that I'd said you were *one of the leads*, not *the* lead.'

'So … you lied too?' I said with a small smile.

Mum wiggled her finger at me. 'Don't push your luck.'

I sighed with relief and took a step back towards the dressing-room. 'Thanks Mum, and I really am sorry. Can I go get ready now?'

'Go. But we'll still be having a long chat after the performance about lying, because I'm still pretty disappointed about that part.'

To think I'd almost survived the whole lecture without one mention of the word disappointed. As I made my way back to the dressing-room, I felt like a huge weight had finally been lifted off my shoulders. I was looking forward to going back onstage and enjoying Act Two without a single care in the world.

'What was that all about?' Khalila asked as I entered the dressing-room.

I shrugged off my jacket and began prancing on the spot to warm my legs back up. 'Oh nothing, I just borrowed Mum's lipstick without asking and she thought I'd lost it.'

Khalila raised her eyebrows at Valentina. I could tell she didn't believe me. I just hoped she wouldn't push it any further. 'She also wanted to know if the two of you wanted to go for milkshakes after the show?' I added. Maybe Mum was right. Maybe mixing ballet and friendship wasn't so bad after all.

'What is it with you Aussies and drinking milk at crazy hours of the day?' Valentina asked with a smile.

Khalila rolled her eyes, and impersonating Valentina's voice added, 'Milk is a breakfast food.'

I laughed and shook my head. 'It's called brupper. Look it up.'

'Brupper?' Valentina and Khalila echoed.

'Breakfast-supper. It's the new brunch. It's what the cool people do.' I said with a wink.

28
Valentina

Something had changed in Amelia. As I watched her from side stage, waiting for my cue to enter the Prince's Grand Ball, I felt like I was watching another dancer. The Fairy Godmother opened Act Two with a beautiful solo to introduce Cinderella to the ball. I've always thought Amelia was a great dancer, but watching her now, I realised she was truly spectacular. For the first time ever, I saw her become completely and utterly lost in the magic of the dance. She was being led by her heart, rather than by the complexity of the choreography. I couldn't even tell you if she was doing the steps that Miss Lily had taught her, or even if her feet were perfectly pointed – although I'm sure they were. I was mesmerised by the way she moved and the joy that illuminated her face. Whatever had been holding Amelia back these past couple of months had disappeared.

I was so distracted by Amelia's dancing, that a small gasp escaped me as my carriage began to move towards the stage. It was my turn to arrive at the ball. Amelia waved her wand towards me and smiled. For the first time ever, I didn't question whether the smile was real or not. I could see in her eyes that it was 100 percent genuine. We were finally friends.

All eyes were on me as I climbed out of Cinderella's carriage, accepting Sam's outstretched hand. The stage was completely full of dancers, the air thick with excitement. Everyone had shaken off their nerves and the result made the Grand Ball feel like a real party. Everyone was smiling and having the time of their life, well, almost everyone. Kate and Ava were still sporting their usual sour expressions, but given they were the Stepsisters, that didn't really matter.

Sam led me towards the centre of the stage, the crowd parting to allow us to share our first dance. Dancing with a boy wasn't anywhere near as scary as I once thought it was, although I was glad I couldn't see Papà's reaction in the audience. He was probably horrified to see his young daughter holding hands with a boy!

As Sam guided me through the dance, I felt like an actual princess. It may have had something to do with the sparkling tiara that had been carefully pinned to my head, or the gemstones that covered my pointe shoes. I'd never sparkled so much in my life.

Even the stage lights bounced off my jewelled tutu, sending colourful spots of light twinkling into the audience. It was lucky the ball scene was a happy moment for Cinderella, because there was no way I could have wiped the smile off my face, even if I'd tried.

I had a moment to catch my breath at the side of the stage while Sam performed a series of extravagant jumps, all intended to impress Cinderella. I clapped politely along with the audience.

'You're killing it, girl!'

My smile grew even larger. I didn't even need to turn around to know who had whispered the praise. Only Khalila would break the 'no talking onstage' rule. She was standing at the back guarding my carriage with the rest of the birds.

I rejoined the Prince in the centre of the stage for our final dance. As Sam hoisted me into the air, wowing the audience with the lift we had spent so many weeks perfecting, I knew Cinderella's time at the ball was about to run out. As the sound of the clock striking midnight cut through the music, I couldn't help but feel a tiny bit disappointed. Tonight had been a fairytale and I never wanted it to end.

My family and I came to this country for a fresh start and for better opportunities. For a while, nothing felt right and

I thought we'd made a mistake by coming.

Standing beside the other dancers, I knew we hadn't. All my life I've known the Southern Italians value three things above all else: family, food and tradition. As it turns out, ballet fits nicely into that list because these dancers were now part of my family and I was more than ready to start a new tradition of dancing alongside them.

As we stood excitedly in a line, waiting for the stage lights to be lifted for the curtain call – our final bow – I felt like I was home for the very first time. The Old Town would always hold a special place in my heart, but lucky for me, there was enough room for Australia too. My new home.

I stood between Sam and Amelia in the middle of the front line, surrounded by the other dancers. My stomach was swarming with butterflies, but this time, I was excited, not scared. This had been the best night of my life. Perhaps now Papà would realise just how serious I was about ballet.

'Curtain!' Someone called from side stage.

I grinned as the curtain began to rise. A thunderous applause broke out from the audience causing goosebumps to prickle my skin. We all took a few steps forward together and curtsied. As we straightened up, I glanced around the audience. Finally, my eyes landed on my family. *All of them*. I had deliberately avoided finding them during the performance. It would have been way too off-putting to know where they were seated. Now, it was impossible to miss them. A ballet crowd is usually quite conservative. They clap politely, occasionally yell out '*Bravo*', and that's about it. My family had missed that memo completely. They were all out of their seats, clapping and stamping their feet loudly. I laughed despite my embarrassment. Amelia was probably mortified by their lack of etiquette. As I locked eyes with Papà, he lifted his fingers to his lips and blew a kiss. It was a small gesture but it said a lot. His eyes were twinkling with pride.

I could feel my grin extending all the way up to my ears, maybe even further. I didn't realise I was crying until a wet drop trickled down my cheek.

'*Evviva* Vale!' Caterina cheered, jumping up and down beside Papà. There was one other person who caught my eye. Salvatore. I was surprised to see him wedged between Caterina and Giuseppe. I hadn't expected him to come. We both stared at each other for a moment. I mouthed *grazie*, and he nodded in response, raising his hands high above his head to clap even louder. It had been a funny few months and I'd really missed my brother. It meant a lot to me that he'd come to watch me dance.

All of us dancers took a few steps back, before returning forward for another bow. The audience cheered with even more enthusiasm. I realised the rest of the dancers were looking expectantly at me. Sam grabbed my hand. 'It's our turn,' he said, pulling me towards the front of the stage. I'd completely forgotten the final bow belonged to Cinderella and the Prince. I took a step forward, but then stopped.

'*Un momento*,' I said, dropping Sam's hand.

His eyes widened. 'What are you doing?' he murmured through his smile.

'One moment,' I repeated. I returned to the line and grabbed Amelia's hand, pulling her forward with me.

She looked horrified. 'What are you doing?' she hissed.

'There are two Cinderellas on this stage,' I said. When we reached the front of the stage, I stood proudly between Sam and Amelia.

'Let's do this … *bunheads*,' I said in the most Australian accent I could muster. I looked between Sam and Amelia with a grin.

'Thank you,' Amelia whispered, smiling back.

I pulled Sam and Amelia's hands into the air, before triumphantly taking a very un-balletic bow.

The End

Acknowledgements

I declared I was going to be an author in primary school and got my first official manuscript rejection when I was thirteen from Fremantle Press. It seems only fitting that all these years later, they are now publishing my debut novel.

Thank you to the entire team at Fremantle Press. To Cate Sutherland, my wonderful publisher and editor, thank you for taking a chance on me and for sharing my vision. Thanks also to editor Kirsty Horton, who along with Cate, helped take my treasured manuscript to the next level. To marketing superstars Claire Miller and Chloe Walton, for championing my book. And to Irene King, for the stunning cover illustrations.

To my parents, Tracy and John, for their endless support and encouragement and for the many, many years of dance classes they funded. Special thanks to my mum who used to edit the books I wrote in primary school. You always said I'd be a children's author, I hope it was worth the wait!

To my sister, best friend and cheerleader, Hayley-Marie. You have more faith in me than I'll ever have in myself, and I am so grateful.

My *nonni* migrated to Australia from a small town in Calabria and it's thanks to them that I grew up enjoying big family dinners and traditions like making sauce and sausages on the back veranda. I didn't fully appreciate my part-Italian heritage until I began studying the language and later moved to Italy to work as a nanny. I now consider Italy my second home, largely thanks to my family in the south, and the artificial family that I found while dancing at a small school in Italy's north. *Grazie mille.* You will always have a special place in my heart. Apologies for my inability to translate Italian while dancing.

To my good friend Silvia Burti. *Maestra Silvia,* these days we are separated by more than 13,400 kilometres, but you are always on hand to assist with my now rusty Italian. *Ti voglio tanto bene!* Any mistakes are my own.

To all of the dance teachers I've had over the years, and to those who have danced alongside me, thank you for inspiring me and for making me fall in love with the art. Miss Lily is fictional, but I'd be lying if I said she wasn't inspired by the teachers of my past.

To phenomenal ballerinas Meg Parry and Carina Roberts, thank you for answering my occasional questions and generously giving me an insight into your world.

To my family and friends for their endless encouragement and patience – I'm sure at times you all questioned whether this book actually existed, but regardless, your support was unwavering. Special shout out to my incredible mum's group, who always keep me going when the sleep battery is low and emotions are high. Thank you for keeping me sane, motivated and very importantly, caffeinated.

To those who read early snippets of my book and cheered me on to keep going. In particular, my group of eagle-eye final proof readers – Danielle Halliday, Adam Kett and Hayley-Marie Oladejo. You're all amazing!

Australia's writing community is the best club I've ever been a part of! There are too many writers to name, but thank you to each and every one of you. To those I've interviewed on my podcast, thank you for answering my questions long after the recording has stopped. Your support and advice has been invaluable.

To my cheeky, little man Grayson. You are too young to read this or to understand, but it was thanks to your unpredictably short naps that I learnt to write as if a bomb could explode at any moment. I've somewhat mastered the skill now, so feel free to sleep soundly from now on.

To my faithful writing companion Taco. It's hard to explain how a dog's eyebrows can be judgemental enough to keep you glued to the desk, but big boy, yours are. And I'm so grateful.

My greatest thanks of all goes to my husband, Adam, who despite not sharing my love of books, has dutifully made it his mission to read all of my manuscripts pre-submission and then again pre-publication. Thank you for all of the notes in the margins. For helping me brainstorm plot problems. For the conversations that start in my head and you're forced to decode. For knowing my characters as well as I do and for putting up with my meltdowns – there were many. Most of all, thank you for proudly telling people your wife was a writer, even before I had a published book to my name.

Last but not least, to you, my reader. Thank you for dancing through the pages of my debut novel!

About the author

Chenée Marrapodi is a writer and podcaster, based in Perth, Western Australia. She has a background in journalism and has worked as a reporter for Channel Seven's *Today Tonight*, as well as online news and radio.

Chenée's love of words is rivalled only by her love of dance. Combining the two, *One Wrong Turn* is her first novel.

First published 2023 by
FREMANTLE PRESS

Fremantle Press Inc. trading as Fremantle Press
PO Box 158, North Fremantle, Western Australia, 6159
fremantlepress.com.au

Cover illustration by Irene King.
Cover design by Rebecca Mills
Printed and bound in Australia by Griffin Press.

 A catalogue record for this
book is available from the
National Library of Australia

ISBN 9781760992439 (paperback)
ISBN 9781760992446 (ebook)

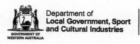

Fremantle Press is supported by the State Government through the
Department of Local Government, Sport and Cultural Industries.

Fremantle Press respectfully acknowledges the Wadjak people of
the Noongar nation as the Traditional Owners and Custodians of
the land where we work in Walyalap.